# SUICIDE EMPIRE

RYAN MOCCASIN

*Edited by*
STEPHANIE FYSH

# SUICIDE EMPIRE

*Take me to a place that it is forever dawn,*

*For it is then I know that I have conquered the night.*

1

Above a broken earth forgotten by time but not by the stars stood the remains of what had once been a vibrant and lively city. Above the dark towers and forgotten ruins stood the black shade of night, from which supernovas, galaxies, and distant suns sprouted forth their heavenly light towards the desolate earth. It seemed a peaceful time, but what shines from afar barely sparkles up close.

Up close, in that hideous city, beneath the bountiful stars, were people who seemed to find hope only in dreams. Few looked up, and as a result, few could interpret the life story of a neutron star. In that time those below searched for understanding but could not decipher what they read in the stars. In that time loss and despair were everyone's daily bread. Loss and despair consumed the social fabric and caused a mighty dark age to descend on what had once been a prosperous land. It became so dark, so clouded, that one could not perceive a single star, a star whose life could affect the very order of things. The life of that neutron star began her night at a subway station in a city called Petersburg. The year was 2051.

The air of this station had a distinct smell of steel dust and long-forgotten food wrappers. Fluorescent lights illuminated the underground cavern. Small pockets of people were scattered around. A busy day was slowly coming to a close, but for one person the night had just begun. She stood by a checkered column facing the tracks. Her long, casual charcoal-color jacket led down toward white shoes. In her left hand, she held onto a cup of coffee; the steam emanated up toward the bright ceiling. In her right hand, she held onto the strap of a brown purse slung over her shoulder.

Above the shoulder was a youthful face ready to be taken on the next leg of her journey. Her eyes were kind, frank, and more green than blue. They were the kind of eyes that said, "*Tell me a story.*"

Her hair gleamed like polished glass in the night and was tied up in a ponytail, regulation for her occupation. She anxiously tapped her purse strap while watching the subway timer count down.

Beneath the charcoal jacket was a navy blue uniform shirt with a small insignia on one side. The insignia portrayed an ominous white tower with an inscription above it that read: "The Complex." Below the insignia was an ID tag. It read: "M. Hopewell—Lead Intern." This had been the woman's life for the past four months. This was the secret identity that she hid underneath her casual jacket. She was still getting used to the one-hour commute from her warm apartment in the westside suburbs of her apartment to the murky outskirts of eastside Petersburg.

In the silent station, Madelyn watched the steam from her coffee cup dance away from her. She began to feel the cool breeze of the incoming subway train. The clock on the timer read 8:00 p.m. as the quiet hum of the tracks grew into a loud screech. The breeze rose into a temperate wind as the train slowed to a grinding halt.

Only one exhausted passenger stepped out across the threshold, sighing deeply, as Madelyn stepped in. She headed toward the back to find her usual quiet spot. Familiar strangers sat scattered through the cream-colored interior, fatigued and staring off into the abyss. The smell of old food was pungent here. Madelyn finding her ceremonial spot, sat down, and waited for the doors to close and the train to depart. When the hush of the doors finally arrived, a monotone voice came over the intercom:

*Passengers. Construction between St. Albert and Cynthia will cause delays of up to forty-five minutes. We apologize for any inconvenience. Passengers...*

Madelyn had already taken her phone out to send a message to her director. In the message she would explain the wonders of the city's construction upgrades. She thought about eventually moving closer to the Eastside.

ON THE SEVENTH floor of the dark, dismal institution called the Complex, the director was organizing the night's marching orders when her phone vibrated. *"Train delay due to construction. Will be late 45 minutes. Sorry! M."*

The electronic screens that surrounded the wide wooden desk stood out in the dim office. The back of the office chair that rose above the director's head had the power and dominion of a throne. The TV monitors that were placed behind it silhouetted her body while her face reflected the bright blue of the electronics. Her eyes were a dark hazel, and deeply focused with a sinister gaze. They were the kind of eyes that said, *"Let me tell you a story."* Dark-rimmed reading glasses pushed her white hair back behind her shoulders. She leaned casually back into the dark throne. The wrinkles around her eyes narrowed as she read the message again.

White light crept through the barely open door. Outside the door was a bright hallway with a gray-tiled floor. Bright light spilled from well-lit offices with their doors yawning wide open. Only one door was fully visible. On the middle of the door was a plaque that read: "Dr. S. Cotham, Director." Inside, Dr. Cotham responded to her employee's message. "*Very well. See you soon,*" she typed.

MADELYN SIGHED as she sat back on the hard plastic seat and pulled her brown purse onto her lap. Her thoughts gravitated toward reading some of the forbidden letters. Her eyes focused on the zipper of her leather bag. She felt the slight vibrations of the train tracks in her feet. All it would take was one small gesture to retrieve the neat pile of handwritten letters. They were only copies of the originals but contained the confessions of minds on the brink of death. They were sacred scripts. And yet she did not know why she kept them in her purse. Perhaps, somehow, they made her feel safe, or powerful. The vibrations beneath the floor strengthened. Her fingers tapped her leg as the temptation of reading also strengthened. But she quickly counseled herself against it. What if one were lost or misplaced? *The people in this train might not understand the patients' dark thoughts, but they would still report the letters to the authorities.*

The train hummed along. The homeless man across from her had almond-colored slacks stained with dirt and a black jacket that led to a torn sleeve. The sleeve led to a hand gripping a bag full of empty bottles. The other hand held the metal pole.

He had sat in the same spot for all the months Madelyn had commuted through the city, blissfully unaware of those around him. He was a great empty companion for her. She enjoyed being a familiar stranger herself. It helped that she was the only employee at the Complex who took this route to work.

Further down the car was a mother who held the handle of a baby stroller. The mother wore a gray wool jacket and a red knitted cap. She slowly rocked the baby stroller and her own upper body. Madelyn could hear the mother sing a distant song beyond the hum of the tracks.

She turned to the window. The tunnel walls were black; every few seconds light gray columns danced by in a blur. She leaned her head against the window and felt the low vibration of the moving capsule. The lights on board illuminated everything around her; it took a few moments for her to notice that the train had exited the tunnel.

The dark blue of the oncoming night painted a black silhouette of the treetops. The mother still sang to the sleeping baby. The homeless man fell under the mother's spell. It was all too enchanting.

And just as Madelyn began to nod off, she felt the train begin to slow down. The vibrations underneath faded. The next station had not yet been called. Madelyn looked out the window and saw flashing blue and red lights coming from ahead, a blurry lightshow unfolding before her. The mother looked up. As their car crawled forward, they both stared out the window. The blur resolved into ambulances and police cruisers surrounding a halted subway train.

*Of course,* Madelyn thought. *The Transportation Department would never mention a death over the intercom, let alone someone who decided to take their own life like that. How horrible!*

The baby awoke crying. But the mother was like a deer

caught in headlights, astonished at the emergency before her eyes, hand over her mouth while watching the flashing lights, and then she quickly turned to her child in the stroller. Madelyn watched as the mother gently pick up the crying baby. The baby cried louder. Madelyn began to feel dizzy from the gravity of it all.

Three police officers surrounded the front of the train, shining their flashlights. They encircled a group of paramedics, who in turn were crouched over a dark object crumpled on the ground. Frantic hands moved to and fro. An unholy gathering was taking place. Madelyn squinted to focus. The halted train's silver exterior was painted with a dark liquid. It peppered the outside of the window and the ground. *Blood*, Madelyn thought.

In the distance, the horizon grew darker; the yellow lights of the halted train illuminated the night. The train itself was empty. *The passengers must have already been escorted off*, Madelyn thought. Perhaps they had taken taxis to the next station. Emergency crews scrambled to erect black curtains around the front of the blood-stained train.

Madelyn slowly sat back down as the train ground to a halt. Everything began to blur. The sound of her own breath overtook all other noise. Her palms began to sweat and she dropped her head into her hands. Nothing remained in her mind but shadows of memories.

She could see her.

She was a young girl again and she could feel her.

She could hear her mother's deep breaths as she leaned against her bedroom door. It was barely open but she could see her lying on her side. The afternoon sunlight barely pushed through the shades. Blankets were scattered on the floor. She lay there, facing away from the door, holding a pillow. The breathing continued its gloomy symphony.

On the nightstand were the pills. Next to the pills were

sepia-toned photos and stacks of books. She loved to read in her former days. She also loved those photos in her former days. Madelyn watched her shoulders rise and then fall with the sound of distant breath. There lay her mother, or rather, a shell of her mother.

Three days later they would find her. Not in her bedroom—she was outside somewhere. She left a note with messy handwriting. Her writing had always been neat and orderly. The uneven, unfinished sentences were the portrait of a life broken and diminished.

Madelyn remembered the old blue sweater they found her in when she washed up on shore. She remembered the questions the authorities asked her—fairly standard for the day and age they lived in. *Not many people make it over the barricade*, she overheard one of them say to another. Madelyn remained stoic and calm throughout, until she made it back home and crumpled into a ball by her mother's door. She cried waterfalls for her mother.

There was no breathing on the other side of the door, in her mother's room. There was only hideous silence. The government officials seized the handwritten note, giving Madelyn no chance to read what was left behind in the mind of her mother. All victims and their belongings were government property. It was part of the new world order that sought to erase the glorification of "independent methods," as they were called.

The only thing Madelyn had salvaged was an old sepia photo that was now nestled deep within her brown purse. Madelyn pushed back against the memories. She pushed back against never knowing what that handwritten letter said.

Slowly she opened her eyes and regarded her current surroundings, wondering if the dream sequence was over.

The flashing lights slowly receded out the rear window

as their train began to hum beneath her white shoes. She looked down; the coffee had spilled beside her feet. By now, the spectacle was a distant blur behind them. Her mind began to gather clarity as the train picked up speed.

The homeless man leaned in toward her. "Miss? You okay? You don't look so well."

"Yes—I'm fine. Just tired from a long day. Thank you."

"The day is just beginning for you, isn't it."

"I guess you can say that." She nodded and looked out the window.

"I mean, only people with a night shift drink coffee at eight-thirty in the evening. Do you work at a hospital or something?" His voice was raspy yet smooth and comforting.

"I guess you can say that, too." A warmth within turned into a smile on her face.

"So all that noise back there probably made you anxious to go out there and help, huh?"

*Is this man a therapist or something?* she thought. "Any emergency would make someone feel compelled to help, I suppose," she said.

"In today's day and age, help is a rare thing to come by. It's no wonder people choose to take their own way out like that." He shook his head and stared out the window. "If only there was an easier way..."

Madelyn regarded the old man as he leaned over and, as if automatically, began to count his empty bottles.

"Yeah," she sat back and took a deep breath. "If only."

The mother's distant song rose over the hum. Madelyn looked over; the mother was rocking the baby stroller. Madelyn began to wonder about the final few minutes of that person's life behind them, and about how awful it must have been to spend them all alone. In that person's final moments, was there a time of peace or one last second of terror? Was it how her mother felt?

These were questions that she was trained to ask herself and her colleagues.

Madelyn's stop was announced. She grabbed her purse and thought about moving closer to the Eastside in order to avoid any more transportation delays. One more taxi ride and she would finally be at work.

**2**

———

The shades of night filled the starless sky. A cold wind danced through the black spruce, causing a distant whistle and a faint rustle in the leaves overhead. The Complex stood firm among the shadowy forest trees. The concrete building was seven stories tall with square windows illuminated by yellow light from inside. A notable feature of the structure was the absence of third-floor windows. Nothing would be illuminated between the second and fourth floors. It was a blank canvas, a mystery waiting to be unravelled. Dark blades of grass surrounded the building's perimeter. The air above smelled of fresh spruce and recent rainfall. In the center of the building was a metal entranceway. From these metal doors a concrete path led away to the paved road. A small white fence drew parallel lines alongside the walkway.

Lights from an oncoming vehicle brightened the trees. The quiet sky was punctured by the closing of a car door. After paying her fare, Madelyn smiled at the driver then turned to take stock of the ominous surroundings. Her smile dissolved. The cold breeze kissed her face; the trees shuddered and moved with the wind. After a long sigh she began to walk toward the shadowy building. Her gaze wandered up to the seventh floor.

~

THE BALEFUL EYES of Dr. Cotham were intensely focused on her TV monitors. She watched Madelyn walk toward the entrance. She had been given extraordinary privilege to monitor from this office every movement in the facility, save for a few confidential spaces. And she had developed a certain fondness for the new intern. Madelyn had come to the Complex with sparkling reviews from the Psychology department at the University of Petersburg. But it was not her credentials that were most interesting. It was her sincere, almost childlike interest in anyone she spoke with. Her warm emerald eyes invited others to be themselves with her. Dr. Cotham held wonderful hopes for what the young woman could bring to the research division of their growing program.

~

MADELYN FELT eyes watching her as her feet tapped quietly on the concrete. She began to feel the weight of it all as she pushed the heavy entrance door. The metal detector hummed quietly as she walked through, her purse strap over her shoulder. On the brick wall by the security office, the digital clock read 9:30 p.m—a half-hour later than usual. Her steps took on a faster cadence. *No time to recuperate in the locker room*, she thought.

Her white shoes echoed throughout the lobby. The security guard nodded to her as he handed over a set of key tags that would grant her entrance to every floor except the third. She then made her way to the elevator, stepped in, and pushed the button for the sixth floor. Those emerald eyes stared forward as the doors closed. She let out an elongated sigh.

~

Dr. Cotham watched Madelyn rise in the elevator. The young lady, so quickly promoted to Lead Intern, gave her hope that the program would be in good hands when they expanded their presence. The tardiness of the night shift was usually handled with an iron fist, but she would give Madelyn a lighter touch. The director grabbed her notes, walked out of the dark office, and headed for the sixth floor to dole out the night's marching orders to the interns.

~

"That was certainly an interesting choice of terrain for last night's final programming," said Errol Winters, junior chemist in the Scientific Department.

"I was surprised the AI left it in. It was my last-second suggestion to the program," replied Jose Pratts, junior architect in the Technology Department.

"And the director had no qualms?" asked Errol.

"Didn't even flinch. See, that's how upper class my architectural taste really is. Stick with me and one day we will have an office on the penthouse floor."

"Either that or a cell on the third floor," Errol replied grimly.

"You don't even know what the third floor looks like—none of us do." Jose's smile was sinister.

"Perhaps you can build one for us—you seem to have good taste." They both smirked as they stepped up to the meeting room's glass entrance. The hush of the automatic doors punctured the quiet air.

Inside the meeting room was a certain unease. The nightshift was starting late, making the department interns anxious about the meeting ahead of them. Madelyn sat near the end of the oval table opposite the entrance, with five other psychologists. They wore the navy blue uniforms of recorders and analysts. Beside them were four junior chemists with an empty chair among them. The chemists sat beside four other digital architects who were busy discussing new programs among themselves. There too was an empty chair.

As Jose and Errol found their seats, a few eyes nervously looked at the clock. The blue numbers read 9:45 p.m. The room was brightly lit but cool, like a brisk walk along the shoreline at dusk—cold, but somehow comfortable. This temperature was maintained throughout the building, no matter how many people were jammed into a room. It also smelled of strong coffee. In fact, that was the lifeblood of this place: caffeine. It usually took a few months and some counseling for fresh employees to grasp the nightly routine. The counseling was mandatory.

In that age, therapy sessions were conducted by a quantum computer that specialized in human interactions and in calculating the sum of people's emotions. This highly advanced artificial intelligence could sort through intangible variables and extract a tangible outcome, or "course to action," for its subjects. The early versions of the software were developed by pioneering psychologists, after which a pilot program was agreed upon. The overseers and engineers of therapy AI referred to it as the Frontier of Advanced Therapy and Experiments, or FATE. The FATE program was deployed as a tool to dig deeper into the human mind.

It was this program that was used in all the Complex's counseling sessions, including for the patients.

The interns were quietly chatting around the conference table when the lights dimmed. The chatter quickly dissipated as Dr. Cotham entered the room. The glass doors hushed to a close.

"Okay, everyone, please refer to the agenda in front of you," the director said sternly. Her voice expressed frustration. "I will have to make this quick. As you have seen on the agenda, three patients are scheduled for the Mirage program tonight. It's business as usual—nothing should be out of the ordinary. But I want to talk about two other things before we go out there." Her voice now became calm and steady. She moved around the side of table to the middle of room and pointed to a hovering image that began to rise from the center of the oval table, where the projector was. All fourteen bodies seated around the table leaned toward to the hologram. From where Madelyn sat, she saw only a paragraph of words with an image below it.

Dr. Cotham continued. "This group of men before you are from the Department of Human Capital. All of them are familiar with our aims; the directors want to show them how their funds are being put to use. They will be sitting in on tonight's Mirage program."

With a gesture, she enlarged the image. It showed three old men with brown tweed suits and salt-and-pepper hair, each of them holding a briefcase. They looked like oddly built clones of each other. Their expressions were uninterested and aloof. Madelyn began to wonder if they were prepared to see the inner workings of the Complex first hand. *Perhaps their innocence will be shaken indefinitely.*

"As you can imagine," the director said, "they are far out of their element by visiting us at night, but it is an important procedure. So please continue to be accurate and astute when cataloguing your findings. Be prepared for questioning from any of these government officials, and"—her voice grew stronger—"be prepared for interviews to be on the record."

Madelyn glanced around her; a few interns seemed apprehensive about this new development. She moved her gaze to one of the junior chemists. He sat across from her: square shoulders, short brown hair swept to the side, a handsome beard, and a dark jacket with a tag above the right breast that said "E. Winters—Junior Chemist." His sapphire blue eyes wandered toward her, as if he knew somehow that he was being watched. He gave Madelyn a warm smile of acknowledgment.

Madelyn was suddenly conscious of how in their private correspondence they had shared confidential information about the patients—on her part, the letters. This she had done in order to appease Errol's blooming interest. He was not given the same access to information as the psychologists, and he had asked Madelyn, desperately, if he could know what was in the mind of the patients in their final days. Sharing a few of their handwritten letters had helped placate his murderous curiosity.

It had also helped justify the time he spent formulating the exact amount of chemicals needed when the patient was in final staging. He was allowed to access only a patient's physical makeup, and he thirsted to understand their minds and souls.

The hologram of the government officials dissolved in front of them. Dr. Cotham turned a dial on the wall and everyone's face became more visible. The air seemed to grow warmer. Dr. Cotham walked to the side of the table and took a deep breath.

"Now, on to the next item on the agenda," she said with a sigh. "Those of you in this room do not have clearance to speak face to face with the patients or to know what happens on the third floor, save for a few who need to from time to time." She began to circle the conference table. "This is to ensure the utmost objectivity when building our portfolios. But it has come to my attention that a few of you cannot seem to keep your curiosity at bay." She looked over at the group of psychologists. "For the information of those who do not have access, your job is to extract and analyze the thoughts that race through the patients' minds. Nothing more. From there, we can paint a picture for them while they experience the final stage of the Mirage program." She leaned forward with hands spread on the conference table. "All this information contributes to our scientific endeavors. The Compassion Labs and Experiments—COMPLEX—was built to better understand the human mind. You are part of this journey."

Jose looked over at Errol and shot him a sarcastic smirk. They had heard this sermon many times before.

But Dr. Cotham immediately focused in on Errol. "Is there something you would like to add?" Her aggressive tone shook the room.

"Um, no, ma'am. Just nervous for the government visit is all," he said timidly.

"Well, you have no reason to be if you remain disciplined and pay attention to your work."

Errol nodded and sunk lower in his chair. Jose smiled.

Dr. Cotham shifted her weight as she leaned away from the table. "Our record keeper, Ms. Cross, has brought it to my attention that there have been some anomalies in the catalogues submitted to her."

*Ms. Cross?* Madelyn thought. *Oh yes, Eliza Cross. An old bat in the body of a middle-aged woman. Certainly, nothing in this world would please her more than seeing us disciplined and fired.*

"We have just under one hundred and fifty employees in the Complex," the director continued, "all but a few of whom seem to understand our goals and objectives. The point is this: We are given extraordinary privilege to conduct this work for the public good. And if the information and data we extract are compromised because a few of you cannot remain professional, then what will that do for future research? These things *cannot happen*. No information is to be shared across departments in the internship program. Not under my watch." She turned to the chemists.

Madelyn's stomach began to turn and she squeezed her hands together on the agenda in front of her. This had to be a direct aim at the correspondence between her and Errol. It was warning fire.

"We have a mandate to grow the Mirage program in a responsible manner," the director continued. "This includes building a disciplined team of scientists, psychologists, and architects through a robust and healthy internship program. We do not want any surprises or the whole program will be discontinued. Is this understood?"

Madelyn looked up from her clenched hands. Around the room, the interns nodded in agreement. Over where the chemists sat, Errol sent a gentle smile in Madelyn's direction. After the meeting, she hoped to ask him a few questions regarding what had just transpired.

The lights became dim as Dr. Cotham dismissed everybody and ordered them to prepare for the first programming of the night. The clock on the wall read 10:00 p.m.

## 3

___

Madelyn sat in the locker room staring at the floor, her head in her hands. The lights were off but inside her mind was a brightness that was searching for answers. *Have I gone mad? It's foolish to get upset about the trivial, minute operations of this place.* But she wasn't the only one worrying about them. *Maybe Dr. Cotham is going mad, not us,* she thought.

As a psychologist, she had developed a habit of writing down in detail what was causing her anxiety. She had already begun to paint her time on the subway train in words into her digital journal on her phone. Phrases and sentences would help release her from the slump she found herself in. The smell, the lights, the vibrations—everything would be detailed. As she tapped a few buttons on her phone to check her messages, she heard a soft knock on the door.

"Madelyn, it's me," came the gentle voice of Errol. "I saw you walk down here twenty minutes ago and was wondering if you're okay. We all need to be in prep soon."

"Okay," Madelyn said as she placed her phone in her

brown purse and put it in her locker. "Just checking a few messages."

Her white shoes made the slightest noise as she walked toward the door. When it opened, she found him standing there, leaning against the wall with his arms crossed. She gleaned a look of genuine concern from his sapphire blue eyes.

She was right. Deep down inside, Errol knew, he was beginning to develop an attraction to her. He wished to one day find paradise alongside her, but there was a yawning chasm between them: the institution they worked at forbade any intimacy between their employees. And there was also the mystery of who Madelyn really was, what she was really all about. For someone so sincere and warm in conversation, she maintained a cryptic aura about her. She wore her privacy like a crown and seemed to take comfort in keeping people in the dark, or across her own chasm that, Errol thought, would never allow her to open up intimately to him. Yet he took solace in their work-related conversations, and she seemed to do the same.

"Well," she said. "It seems we have startled the powers that be."

"We should have refrained from using their systems to communicate." Errol stood up from the wall. "God knows they love to linger in people's personal lives."

"Then again, so do we."

"That much is true. Privacy has become an ancient relic around here."

"A lot of things have, Errol. It's a new world."

"But I must say—you don't look yourself tonight. You seem ill at ease."

"The close call in the meeting didn't help," she said, crossing her arms and looking at the ground. They started down the corridor. "There was an incident on the way here," she added solemnly. "I was late today because someone decided to jump in front of a subway train."

"*Your* train?"

"Not ours, but a different one. The police and paramedics were everywhere. I haven't seen that in years."

"It's startling to hear that it still happens out there," he said solemnly.

"Yeah. Perhaps this world isn't so new after all."

"Does Dr. Cotham know about it?"

"I haven't told anyone but you. I'm sure they'll find out soon enough."

"They will." He looked at her. "It must have caught you off guard."

"You know, I study this kind of thing all the time within these walls. But this incident challenged me."

"How so?" he asked.

"I don't really know. Perhaps it's a little bit of karma coming around to show me something. But that doesn't change what happened. It just made me... question things." She bit her lower lip and looked back down.

"That seems perfectly natural. It's perfectly human. You should be concerned if it happens and you feel nothing at all. You have an extraordinary gift for seeing other people, Madelyn." She looked back up and his sapphire eyes met hers.

The emptiness inside her seemed less of a distraction than it had. Their warm conversations always seemed to allay any bitter feelings about the job before her. But this was the end of the hallway.

"Thank you, Errol," she said. "Can we talk again during coffee break? I need to pick your brain about a few things."

"Absolutely."

He then smiled and they parted ways, Madelyn on by elevator toward the fifth floor, where her department was, and Errol down another hall to the ground-floor break room to grab a coffee.

In between, on the third floor, they both knew, the patient was getting ready for programming. And on the seventh, Dr. Cotham stood in front of her monitors and watched them walk away from each other. A slight grimace appeared on her face.

MADELYN PRESSED five then watched the floor numbers change on the screen overhead. It went from ground to two, and then it skipped a number. At four she felt the floor slow down. Her body lightened. Someone, she knew, was waiting on the other side of the metal doors. The world seemed to slow down as the doors pushed away from each other.

They stared at each other as long-time enemies do. Ms. Cross was wearing her usual black uniform. Her beady eyes regarded Madelyn with little respect and much hatred. Nothing was said as she entered the elevator and stood beside Madelyn. Her thin, pale fingers pushed the seventh-floor button. The floor began to pick up speed. Out of the corner of Madelyn's eye, she could see the black hair pulled tightly into a ponytail, the warlike stance of the old bat disguised as a middle-aged woman. The silence was deafening.

As the floor once again slowed down, Ms. Cross slowly looked over at her.

"No surprises tonight." Her voice was high and mighty. Every time she spoke, it felt like an order from a general in wartime.

"Of course," replied Madelyn. "I have heard of tonight's royal visit from the government. Should be a good show." The doors hushed open. She nodded as she stepped out.

"We will find out where the leaks are coming from, Ms. Hopewell. Whoever it is will be dealt with accordingly." Madelyn turned around. The woman forcefully pushed a button. The doors hushed closed with both of them glaring at one another.

Madelyn turned back and headed down the hallway. She felt as if she needed a bath in holy water. *Such a cruel woman! So what if they find out? I'll say it was for further research. Dr. Cotham should understand*, she thought.

Finally she was at her computer station, ready to record the data from the night's proceedings. On her screen were graphs, formulas, and numbers compiled by the department's cognitive psychologists. The data indicated the mental activity of the patient prior to the night of programming and what was to be expected. Interns and lower-level employees were not given access to a patient's full records, only allowed to monitor physical and mental vitals. The patients were kept under lock and key, accessible only to Dr. Cotham and her closer associates.

Madelyn opened another window. This one displayed handwritten letters. The patients wrote them during the first few days of their intake. After they were processed, days or weeks of talk therapy sessions with FATE would follow, in which emotional traits and psychological values would be assigned to the patient. A few questions here and further inquiries there would eventually result in an informed character sketch for the directors above.

The information extracted from the dire letters would be analyzed and reanalyzed by the powers above in order to create a dream world for the patient. The architects would be heavily involved in designing that world, but ultimately it was artificial intelligence that guided the process.

She opened up window after window until she found what she was looking for. It was one of the first letters written by the first patient who would be going through programming tonight. It had no title.

*Still here. After many failed attempts, they finally answered my call. If I wasn't sleeping, I was crying. There didn't seem to be a moment when my own mind wasn't against me. Everything was a distant blur, including my thoughts and memories. I was afraid to feel anything because in those darkest moments, all my emotions seemed weaponized against me. It felt like the wolves were always at my door. Reality was coming for me, and she had fangs for teeth. The whole world seemed on fire and ablaze at the end.*

*It was as if I was always in fight-or-flight mode. Fear gripped me at all times.*

*Reality wanted to leave me like dead leaves on the ground. I was always imagining falling from the treetops like one of those leaves. It felt like it was always raining dead things in my mind, and I was one of them.*

*Up until today, crowds made me feel lonely. If I had any hope, it hid under a rock my whole life, never showing itself to me.*

*They tell me there is paradise in this place. An artificial thought. I feel like a lab rat in this odd institution.*

*Why is their hope is so inflated? Everyone here seems suspiciously unfazed by the task they are given. It too seems artificial. Perhaps I am just not used to this environment.*

*Nothing seems to help, not even my meds. And so I am left alone in a busy institution. The emptiness has consumed me. A dark mist still floats around my feet. Some days it almost swallows me whole and then I have difficulty breathing. If I try to climb, I look up to see a much darker cloud.*

*Nothing shines in the fields of my soul. It is a wasteland. This world is a wasteland.*

*Nothing seems pure because everything is haunted. Haunted by my own thoughts. The suffering, it eats me. It pulls me apart. I beg for the demons to let me go, and let me breathe.*

*And in this place, this room?*

*They tell me there is peace. I do not believe them.*

MADELYN STOPPED TO BREATHE. But as she closed the letter and then the digital folder entitled "Patient 1258," her heart raced. The patient was the one thousand two hundred fifty-eighth person recommended to the Mirage program.

At that moment, Madelyn knew, the patient was stationed in a waiting room on the third floor. The fifteen-by-fifteen-foot sanctuary had dark concrete walls with a white-tiled floor. In the middle was a chair attached to a platform. Only the white lamp that hung at the center of the room illuminated the still chamber. The room had been designed to allow the patient to enjoy their final thoughts before the Mirage program began, a moment which would be signaled by the opening of a door at the far end of the room.

She knew this because Errol and Jose knew this. *I'm not the only one sharing secrets in this place,* she thought.

At that moment, Madelyn knew, the patient was sitting there, waiting for the final call. And she knew that Dr. Cotham was watching the night's programming. She would be watching tonight along with the government officials from her seventh-floor office.

Jose was preparing architectural procedures on the sixth floor; Errol was on the fourth floor watching the countdown to 11:00 p.m. on the digital clock, ready to take notes. Everyone in the building was preparing for what would be happening on the third floor, the one without windows.

**4**

———

In the holding chamber on the third floor, the body of a young woman cast a shadow on the tiled ground. The white lamp hanging overhead lit the whole chamber. The patient sat in a metal chair with her head down. On her body she wore a tattered wedding dress. Above the chest were no straps, just remnants of them and bare skin. The now-fringed hem of the dress barely touched the floor in front of her. The fabric was pearly white with hints of blood and stains peppered throughout. The patient sat there like the queen of her own dominion, powerful and ready for what was to come next.

Dead silence hung in the air. Only the long, slow breaths of the patient filled the emptiness of the gray room. No electronics distracted the patient from her lonely thoughts. No cameras or recorders arrested the attention of the person waiting for her final call. The empty air was gentle and temperate against her skin. Her longing eyes glanced around the small sanctuary in which she waited. They settled in front of her on a black door with a window in the middle. The glass was also black.

In the gray stillness, a yellow light began to form in the

window of the black door. And then her final call came: a click followed by the shush of air escaping a room. The white lamp above her chair turned off.

The patient didn't turn to look at it; she gleamed ahead to see the black door slide to the side. A dim yellow light began to steal away the dimness from the chamber. The patient stood up; she felt compelled to walk through the door that had just opened. Slowly, her bare feet moved her across the smooth, warm floor. Both of her hands reached out to grab the steel doorframe. She leaned over the threshold and peered in. The larger room was much fresher and hotter than the enclosed space she had been sitting in.

The air within the larger chamber was filled with a yellow fog. She glanced up and around, trying to discern what was in it, but she was unable to see clearly. She took an uncertain step forward but kept one hand on the doorframe. Her deep breaths began to shorten as she let go and walked in.

The room smelled like a warm spring day, like the perfume of blossoming flowers. As she took a few more steps, she looked back. Beside the door was a black button with no sign over it, though she knew what it was meant for.

Slowly, she lifted her hand to the button, took a deep breath, and pushed it. She heard a click and suddenly the door had shut and the window had faded to a dark gray. And then the floor was soft, a material she could not place a label on. She had become so used to concrete or tile floors that her own feet were confused. At this moment, she was suddenly overcome with an enchantment that seemed to assuage her confusion. The atmosphere of this alien place had taken her.

The yellow fog felt as if it was hugging her, and this encouraged her to keep walking. As she moved softly along, the yellow fog dissolved into a white cloud until all of it slowly began ascending to the sky. The haunting drift upward began to reveal her new surroundings.

She was now standing in a forest. The trees around her were past their summertime glow. There were brown shades of fir and towering bodies of oak trees. The leaves were orange and brown and barely hung onto their branches. The daylight barely cut through the treetops. She turned around; a few rays of sunlight danced around the enchanted forest. Somewhere birds were whistling and chirping the day away.

The forest floor was covered in brown dirt, with small piles of leaves everywhere. It smelled of cool, fresh air. It passed through her nostrils and lifted her spirits. She had not smelled the fresh fall air in a very long time. An ominous feeling of being watched haunted her mind. It was the feeling of being alone but also of a supreme being stalking her soul. She buried this idea.

The nightly terrors of her former life seemed to fade away. Her eyes wandered down to the scars on her arms. *Battle wounds*, she thought. After a first step on the forest floor she felt a sudden urge to wander, to explore, to run free. Her dress danced in the breeze. Rays of light caressed her skin.

After running a few steps, she bent down to run her hands through the cool soil. There was life in this place. She walked over to an oak tree and ran her hand along it. The surface felt alive. It felt of a whole new world opening itself up to her. Then a branch snapped. It rang out from close behind her. She turned slowly.

And when she finally saw what was stalking her, she let out a quiet scream. The dark gray beast stood calmly with its glassy black eyes fixated on her. Its mouth was closed. Its chest cavity moved slowly with its deep breaths. It did not move a muscle yet it seemed madly curious about the woman before it.

The patient remembered that this was all an elaborate mirage, so she stood where she was. Yet her heart began to race as she stared at the beautiful beast before her, its muscular body towering above the forest floor.

The wolf began to wag its tail as it stepped closer. It let out a soft and gentle grunt as it took a few more hesitant steps toward the patient. Yet she felt no fear. She felt a certain fondness in the wolf for her. When it reached her side, it licked her fingers.

She raised her hand and ran it along the wolf's head. The creature stood just above her chest, and it was as majestic in life as it was in pictures. She was held in wonder by the love and care it gave her. She leaned down and it began to lick her face. Tears welled in her eyes as she wrapped her arms around the wolf's neck. It was so soft and warm... Its peaceful demeanor calmed her heart.

Her spirit was so used to making an enemy of this crea-ture. It was a metaphorical threat that she had faced every day of her previous life. *Reality was coming for me, and she had fangs for teeth*, she thought with her arms wrapped around the beast's neck. *But not today*, she thought. Her spirit felt at one with the wolf. She continued to cry as the beast comforted her.

After some time the wolf began to pull away. She stood up and looked to where it turned. Above her, she noticed, the leaves were beginning to fall. She caught one in her hand and felt the brittle skin of it against hers. One by one, leaves fell all around her. So she began to walk alongside the wolf. Her wedding dress kept her warm as she followed wherever the beast would take her. The falling leaves only added enjoyment to their new adventure. The daylight stayed overhead while the fall air gave her new life and meaning.

The wolf was picking up a scent. The beast's muscular legs led their way through the enchanted forest. Birds sang their song. The trees dropped their leaves all around the two companions as they ran through the forest. Suddenly they reached the end of the forest and ran out from its edge.

The smell had not changed, but now she was standing in a green meadow. What had once been a season of organic materials perishing back to the earth became a world full of new beginnings and bright colors. The evolutionary change from death to life compounded her euphoria in this alien world. Nothing seemed to be a threat, and everything seemed to be a promise. The promise was that no harm would occur but that peace would be delivered. She felt in her bones that she deserved infinite peace. And in this fresh landscape, it was given to her.

In the distance she began to hear the haunting sound of orchestral music. Strings and harps were the quiet soundtrack to her newfound environment. The soft material of the floor began to change texture until it felt like blades of grass kissing the bottom of her feet. She knelt down to brush her hands through the green foliage, and a sigh of relief took her breath away.

*Life*, she thought.

A slight breeze caressed her pale skin. Up past the meadow another forest edge revealed itself to her; trees surrounded the green meadow. The forest opened itself up all around this haunting, beautiful place, trees of white oak and pine spreading across her field of view. Above the trees was a bright blue sky with a sun that spoke of daylight and peace.

Then she looked down at her body. Her right arm touched all of the scars on her left forearm and she was surprised to feel the warmth of her own touch. For an eternity it had seemed that she had gone cold and lived in an eternal winter. In this place the seasons seemed to move in reverse.

Looking down beyond her arms and legs she perceived something strange. There, in the green grass, a dark mist began to gather around her feet. It did not threaten to swallow her like the many other times, in her room. She turned around to see the wolf ten feet away. It let out a slight whimper and turned to run. She understood this as the beast's time to exit. After watching the wolf disappear back into the trees, she turned around to watch the haunting spectacle unfold.

This time the dark mist had a welcoming aspect. And then it started to lead somewhere. The dark mist began to grow a path away from the forest edge. It proceeded to dance along the soft grass toward the middle of the green meadow. It was all too mesmerizing for her. All around, flowers began to spring up. Birds chattered away. She began to follow the path that was being drawn for her. Each step felt as soft as pillows. Then, looking further ahead, she saw what the dark mist was leading to.

In the middle of the green meadow there had appeared a small, brown cottage with a white roof. It had a wooden door with a window to one side. The daylight shone down on the cottage as if to welcome any troubled traveler to go in and find rest. Her feet led her toward the cottage, the dark mist still dancing all around her. The music raised a sense of wonder in her mind, and she walked ever more softly toward the door. The sweet smell of lavender reached her nose. Finally her feet stopped a few steps away from the cottage.

In that quiet place, the patient spoke out a quiet "Hello?" but was met with nothing. She stepped closer to the door and reached for the metal knob, and as she did, the music began to fade. She looked back; the green meadow was undisturbed save for the path she had carved out with her own feet. The dark mist had disappeared.

As she turned the knob and opened the door, it let out a slight creak. Her warm hands held onto the doorframe while a bright new room swept itself into view. The room was the size of the whole cottage, with wooden walls and floors. Her gaze immediately gravitated to the wooden table in the center. On the table was a dark red book that resembled a bible or a songbook. Beyond the table was a fireplace with a few logs burning. The crackle of the fire filled the empty air. From outside it was joined by the distant whistles of birds. The smell of lavender had disappeared; this room smelled of campfire and spruce. And in her heart it had the odd sense of being home, a feeling she had been deprived of for many years.

*Could this be the place where I start fresh and new?* she thought.

She let go of the doorframe. The wooden floor was warm to her feet. Every groove and imperfection seemed magical to her. She stepped toward the table with her eyes fixed on the book. It was leatherbound with no discernible words on the cover, but a thin book, with only a few pages. The daylight from outside glared on the wooden floor beside the table. She ran her warm hands over the dark red cover.

Her left hand began to open the front cover, revealing a blank first page. The pages were very thick and they were the color of white ivory. On the second page was a photo of balloons. The photo was black and white but it generated a feeling of excitement within the patient. Something was happening to her that she had not felt in a very long time.

She was unable to put a word on it, so she kept turning to see what else was in the book.

On each page were photos of what seemed to be someone else's life. These were pictures of strangers. She leaned in to study their faces. No connection was made in her mind, but in her heart grew a strong sense of warmth and comfort. These were strangers yet they were *familiar* strangers, like people you share a morning commute with. It gave her so much joy to see them.

*That's the word*, she thought. *Joy!*

These strangers in the book gave her new meaning: a young woman enjoying a music class; someone's first pet; a plane ride to a distant land; a green meadow. She did not recognize the faces, but these strangers did not torment her soul. The more pages she turned, the more her tears fell onto the table.

Placing a hand to her mouth, she turned toward the fire. A bed had appeared. It had a great number of blankets and pillows. The fire still crackled as she carefully shut the book, lifted it from the table, and looked around. The cottage was warm and comforting. She conceived a desire to rest on the bed by the fire and reflect on the beautiful images she had just seen. As she stepped closer, she ran an open hand along the warm, soft blankets. She sat and then lay down in her wedding dress, hugging the book close to her chest. The bed felt like a soft cloud; it enveloped her in a warm embrace.

More tears ran down her cheeks, tears of joy, and they washed away all of her pain, all of her suffering. She breathed deeply. The world seemed to fold itself into a beautiful and harmonious state of equilibrium. Deep breaths punctured the soft air in the cottage. A great tiredness began to wash over her soul. Breath by breath she moved deeply within herself.

Then a breath turned to a yawn. And outside the

daylight began to diminish as the green meadow turned dark.

Inside, she curled up with her book. She felt a perfect peace. She felt a world full of infinite bliss descend upon her. She did not feel lonely anymore.

She closed her eyes and fell into a deep sleep. Inside, the cottage grew dark except for the dancing of the flames in the fireplace. Outside, the birds sang their final song and kissed the day goodnight. The patient's breaths became a slow hush.

After a few minutes, her chest stopped moving. Her world stopped moving. The flames in the fireplace slowly faded out of existence.

5
_______

The government officials flanked Dr. Cotham, watching the TV monitors. With tweed suits and awestruck expressions, the older gentlemen remained composed throughout.

The lights in her office were dimly lit, as usual. On one screen was a feed of the Mirage room in which the patient spent her final moments. It was a large rectangular room with white walls and padded flooring. The camera, installed in the upper corner, slowly zoomed in on the middle of the chamber. There in the middle of the silent tomb lay the pale body of a young woman. She was slightly curled up, with her arms hugged around her chest; she wore a tattered wedding dress. From the view of the camera in the corner, one of the officials could make out a slight, peaceful smile forever engraved on the patient's face.

No one spoke for a very long time until the far door of the Mirage room opened. Three people wearing black decontamination suits walked toward the lifeless body in the middle of the floor. The government officials noticed the common insignia on their chests.

"Those are the physicians arriving to confirm the time of

death," Dr. Cotham said as she looked to the clock on the wall. 11:33 p.m., it read. Then she turned to her guests. "Before we head down to investigate the data, are there any questions?"

Dr. Cotham looked forward to their questions. The government officials had been briefed on the strict code of ethics surrounding the nature of the work at the Complex. It had been agreed among all parties that the government visit would be an occasion on which to ensure that the technical details of the program were being carried out in a responsible manner. Dr. Cotham looked forward to showing them the technical labs.

"When the physicians arrive," inquired the more quiet of the three softly, "the room, or the AI that operates the room, knows who these people are?"

"The Mirage room is equipped with sensors and cameras that, when the program is running, watch for and respond to movements," Dr. Cotham lectured. "At the end, it shuts down, allowing the physicians to arrive, although they have to wear suits in case traces of chemicals remain in the air. What you are looking at is one of three Mirage rooms on the third floor. I cannot specify more for security purposes, so that those who may be illegally watching will not know the exact location of the program. But that would impossible with our security parameters."

"Yes," said one official. "What *about* security? I see you are given a bird's-eye view here, which is brilliant. But what if, let's say, the patient developed second thoughts and wished to terminate their programming?"

"As you saw the patient do in the video feed," Dr. Cotham explained, "it is the patient who starts the program, by pushing the button. This procedure is discussed with them beforehand many times. Once the program begins, the larger room is on lockdown and the whole system is placed on automatic programming. It's essentially an autopilot that can't be overridden. It would be unbearably disappointing for the patient to find out that they were experiencing a... um... false ending, as it were. The patient is fully aware of what they are doing and also aware of the purpose of the Mirage program. They believe in the program more than we do, I suppose."

The official nodded and looked back at the TV monitor.

"If you have any further questions," Dr. Cotham said, "we can discuss them on the way. Follow me, please." She led them out the door and toward the elevator.

On the fifth floor of the Complex, a group of interns had gathered around a holographic image. They were staring at a picture of a brain surrounded by graphs and numbers. Blues, purples, and greens were seeded in different parts of the brain.

"So much activity in the final moments," said one intern. "I never get tired of seeing it."

Madelyn was off to the side staring into the distance. For her, it was almost mechanical at this point, what they were doing. She had seen over forty of these brain holograms, and each one seemed to lessen the impact of the one before it. But with each a thirst deepened. It needed to be quenched not only by finding the right answers, but by asking the right questions.

Her gaze found its way to the window and outside into the night. She regarded the many stars in the sky. Here, just outside of the city, it was possible to see further out into the heavens. She stared out into the chaotic eternal, wondering about the stars and the cosmos beyond the bitter earth.

She thought about what she would say when Errol joined her for a coffee in a short while. As she thought about how to broach the subject with him, her gaze turned to the little camera nestled in the upper corner of the interns' lab. She remembered that the government officials would be on their way, and that an interview with her would be inevitable.

The door to the lab slowly opened; Madelyn began typing into her computer. Dr. Cotham and her associates walked in and all eyes shifted to the new faces.

"Good evening, everyone," the director said. "Do not mind us. You are doing important work so we do not mean to interrupt. The officials would like to hear from the lead intern, though. Madelyn, could you step forward please?" she said with a strong sense of admiration for the star pupil.

Reluctantly, Madelyn got up from her desk, grabbed some of her notes, and walked over to the group to appease their blooming curiosity.

"Gentlemen," the director said, "this is Ms. Hopewell. She has been here just a shade over four months and has already proven herself to have strong leadership qualities. Anyway, I am gushing and rambling while also delaying precious time." She turned to Madelyn. "So, in review, we have already investigated the data from the other labs on this floor. Perhaps you can begin by explaining why we gather so many interns for this project."

"Yes, of course."

Madelyn felt her stomach flutter; she was unprepared for this impromptu presentation. *It really has been a long night already*, she thought.

"There are a total of six junior psychologists," she explained, "myself included. We help oversee the process of gathering data, such as brainwave activity and psychological responses to the stimuli during the Mirage program. See here, for example." She showed a clipboard with a graph on it. "Patient 1258 began the program in a relaxed state, until about ten minutes into it there was a sudden spike in the amygdala, indicating a certain degree of fear. But it quickly dissipated. From what we have been told in orientation, the Mirage program is designed to activate all the senses and emotions when the patient is in their final moments. It helps them face their fears and destroy the myth, I guess you can say."

The government officials were disarmed. The way Madelyn spoke felt like an immersive dance or a theater play, and she was the greatest performer of all.

"The work of one psychologist," she said, "is compared to that of the next; this is to ensure that we regard the data with objectivity and without bias. We cross-check this against what FATE has extracted from the patient interviews. My specific job as the lead is to gather all data, edit it accordingly, and file it away into a digital portfolio where the directors can access it for their research." She paused her lecture and calmly shifted her gaze to the small crowd.

The government officials were mesmerized by the inner workings of the lab the way Madelyn explained them. Hers was a warm presence among her cooler colleagues, quietly working at their computers.

"Over here," she continued as she led them to the main computer in the middle of the room, "we have a real-time holographic feed of the patient's brain activity during programming."

The officials gathered around at a respectful distance and watched the brain hovering in the air surrounded by colors and data points.

Dr. Cotham, meanwhile, stayed by the door, watching in awe. *It truly is a state-of-the-art facility,* she thought. There had been little initial funding or interest in building such a cutting-edge facility for them to operate out of, but after pursuing private donors they had finally forged a way forward. And as the suicide rate rose beyond its already epic level, public opinion moved in favor of finding innovative ways to help ease the burden of dealing with so much anguish. The government followed suit, opening the Department of Human Capital, where they would attempt to increase the quality of life by any means necessary. The Complex was one of the first programs they funded, and now, looking at the three-year-old building and her staff, Dr. Cotham could not help but feel proud of what they were doing.

"Ms. Hopewell?" asked one of the officials. "If any of you witnessed anomalies or unforeseen circumstances that would make you challenge your personal beliefs, how would you, as lead intern, deal with the matter?"

Madelyn felt more flutters in her stomach: she knew what the man was asking.

"If there were anomalies," she said, "we would report them as we see them. Our job is to gather what we find with the utmost objectivity. Before we are hired for an internship, it is made clear to us than any ill feelings about the Mirage program would undermine the data we pursue. We must separate ourselves emotionally from the patients' records. The reasons for committing our work to the Mirage program are greater than any personal objections."

This was the oath taken when each intern was hired at the Complex and Madelyn grew in confidence in repeating it to the officials. "We are charged with reporting the facts, and nothing else," she said, and gave a gentle smile to the guests.

This seemed to satisfy the officials; they looked at each other and then to Dr. Cotham, who was standing by the door. They all shook Madelyn's hand and then strode off to the hallway past Dr. Cotham. She smiled at Madelyn from across the room. The inquisition over, Madelyn waited until they had left then ran to her computer to finish the reports.

The review after each Mirage program was designed to

remind interns of the need for confidentiality and agreement with their peers. Every other department report was filed away digitally, but the interns' review was required to be printed, signed, and delivered to the seventh floor by Madelyn as lead.

At this moment, Dr. Cotham and the men on an inquiry were tapping the hallway floor with their dress shoes, the visitors chatting among themselves about the supreme quality of presentation they had just received. The wide hallways and cool air gave the impression that they were visiting a hospital yet was everywhere inviting. They passed closed metal doors and underneath bright fluorescent lights until their leader suddenly took a turn into a dark corridor. The Complex seemed much larger than it had from outside, and every turn they took brought them farther and farther into a dark labyrinth. The officials' lively chatter dissipated as the hallways grew darker and darker. The absence of doors and windows dismayed them. Then, suddenly, their leader stopped and turned around.

Her face grew dark and ominous; the sinister glare in her eyes seemed ready for some sort of great reveal. Silence punctured the odd institution. The dark corridors must have been for the top brass only: not one employee could be found or heard.

Dr. Cotham broke the quiet spell in a whisper. "Gentleman, on the other side of these doors, something of a holy gathering is taking place. You will see for yourself one of the interns undergoing a counseling session by the FATE program. I must admit there some shock at first for people who find employment at the Complex, but these sessions are designed to acclimate them to the new environment. The intern will not see or hear us; we will be behind one-way glass."

The officials stood quiet, but deep down there was a

yearning and an excitement to witness an AI program in action.

"The intern's name," Dr. Cotham said, "is Edith. She has been here for four months and is coming along nicely."

After a wave of her hand in front of the black dial pad to the side, the doors seemed to push away from each other to reveal a black chamber with chairs and a window. It had the air of a movie theater. The four strode into the black chamber. Not a sound could be heard from the speakers. Even their footsteps seemed to be absorbed by the gray sponge-like substance on the walls.

"Soundproofed and air-tight security, gentlemen." Dr. Cotham wasn't whispering anymore. "In here, were have all the freedom we could want to discuss what we are about to see."

The window reflected their own anxious faces back to them. The anticipation was palpable as they all took a seat in brown leather chairs. After a few still moments and another wave of the hand by Dr. Cotham, their reflections dissolved and the counseling room spread out before them.

It was a simple yet aesthetically pleasing chamber—walls with a mosaic of gray and yellow lights slowly dancing like waves, a tall fern with green tassels spread out like tiny arms, a short cherry-colored table with notes and writing utensils on it, and next to all that a Victorian antique chair with flowered upholstery. In that chair sat the star of the show, the celebrity they all awaited.

Edith seemed unmoved by the path that had brought her there. In fact, she seemed acclimated enough for the program. She wore a somber look in her eyes and a slight smirk that almost said, "What are we doing here?"

Her red hair was pulled back, her arms rested on the flowered upholstery, and the rest of her body was covered in a blue uniform, standard for interns in the psychology department.

"She seems incredibly calm," offered one of the officials.

"The challenge of the FATE program is to dive deep into the psyche of the subject—not in a way to break them, but to extract honest and open answers. Although you cannot see them, the room is full of sensors and cameras designed to read physical values. She may seem relaxed, but there are clues that betray that appearance. FATE will find them." Dr. Cotham admired the room before them. She truly did seem to rule this dominion, as if it were her idea that was pioneering everyone into the future.

Edith seemed to understand this while she sat and waited for an incoming voice, a signal that would ease the tension in the air. She seemed to really want this all to be over.

In the silent theater, the mosaic of waves stopped and the lights faded; a dim spotlight lit the antique chair. Throughout the interview chamber and from the speakers in the witness room came a soft and gentle hush. Even the officials felt an incredible peace reveal itself to them. It was a harmony and a voice at a frequency like no other. The voice did not sound like that of a man nor a woman but like that of a celestial being brought forth to understand the world a little bit better.

"Edith," offered the placid and soothing voice of FATE. "How are you today?"

"I am well," she replied. "Certainly better than the first day."

"How so?" The tone of the voice carried a heightened level of empathy.

"I suppose every job has its anxieties on the first day. But every day in this place feels like the first day."

Over the next few silent moments, it seemed as if the AI was calculating a response, but instead Edith continued.

"Yet some days I feel absorbed and unbothered by what's around me in this institution. Perhaps it is circumstantial, though. Perhaps my anxieties are rooted in some personal things going on right now."

"Where in your personal life do you feel these anxieties manifest themselves?"

A deep sigh from Edith reverberated through the dim atmosphere, indicating an introspective moment between the two: a woman and a machine. The officials looked on in wonder at the dramatic play unfolding in front of them.

Edith glared at the fern beside the armchair, and as if something in the green foliage had moved her, she bent over and covered her face with her hands. The emotional dam had broken within her, and she was left vulnerable to those observing on the other side of the glass. A sniff and a tear moved through the speakers.

"FATE...," she sobbed.

"Yes, Edith. Share whatever is on your mind." The machine's voice was disarming. Even the officials felt the urge to share whatever anxieties troubled their spirits.

"Have you ever seen a lunar eclipse?"

"There was one three months ago. We were both working that night."

"That's how it feels sometimes. Before my shift there's a light in my heart to help me navigate the night, but then an eclipse takes all hope and life from me. Is this normal for the other employees?"

"It is not abnormal to feel things like that. I have conducted many of these sessions, and many employees show progress after internship."

"Well, then I suppose I can share something with you that I've been holding onto for a while."

After a slight pause, the play continued.

"Please do. Write it down, if you wish."

Edith wiped a tear from glassy eyes. The spotlight revealed the youthful vigor in her face and the wisdom known only to those who have seen pain. She seemed simultaneously sage and novice. After another long sigh, she sat taller and grabbed the paper and pen. She wrote with a new confidence, as if she was ready to reveal something she had kept hidden for many months. The theater became a confessional in which the officials were the confessors.

But something happened and the window before them dissolved back into a mirror. Edith and FATE were left alone on the other side of the glass, and the officials were left in dismay. The play had come to an abrupt halt.

"It seems we have to end it there, gentleman." Dr. Cotham stood up and towered before her audience of three. "Personal matters must be kept confidential. It was FATE who decided that the window should be closed—that is how ethical the program has become."

"Such an inviting tone! Incredible to see a machine become so advanced," offered an excited official.

"FATE," Dr. Cotham explained, "was calculating in real time the patient's physical response to the questions. Each pause on FATE's part invited the subject to continue. In a way, it knows what patients feel before they say it, and will respond in the most appropriate manner."

"How does one even begin to train it how to respond?"

"By feeding it thousands and thousands of interviews and counseling sessions. Studies from the University of Petersburg show that FATE can diagnose a mental disorder correctly 99.7 percent of the time," Dr. Cotham lectured confidently. "It is much more accurate than humans."

"The voice of FATE seemed euphoric to the common

ear." An official gazed at the window, almost missing the tone he had just heard.

"It trains itself on the best approach for each patient. An advanced AI knows the needs of each patient it interviews, and its memory knows no bounds. As you can see with the eclipse question, it has never seen one but can quickly calculate what one would 'feel' like."

"You are saying that FATE can 'feel' things?"

"It assigns a value to what it perceives, based on algorithms and equations. A sunrise registers higher on the emotional scale than a sunset. FATE not only studies human emotions; it also studies human *experience*. With that knowledge, it can calculate valuable responses faster than a human being."

All three men seemed held in a state of wonder, as if they had just witnessed the frontier of modern medicine. Dr. Cotham continued her lecture on the wonders of advanced therapy while the whole building seemed to breathe in anticipation of the next patient.

Meanwhile, in another room, on the fifth floor, the interns were vigorously completing their reports before the next programming.

After a few anxious moments and a quick tap on the keyboard, Madelyn had printed what they had compiled and made for the hallway. It was a rare occurrence for the director to be out of her office when the intern report was delivered. This thought raced through Madelyn's mind as she carried the portfolio of papers to the elevator.

When her trip to the top floor was done, before enjoying a coffee with Errol in the break room, perhaps she would collect her thoughts in the locker room, alone.

6

Down the sixth-floor corridor, through the many closed doors, sounds of incessant typing on keyboards and into electronic devices punctuated the air. From the entrance into the hallway, Dr. Cotham led the way toward one of the electronic labs.

The director of this department sat at the back of the room. Small reading glasses rested on top of his gray hair. His face portrayed the life of a man in his fifties who always wore the same tan suit with the same dark red tie. On his right chest the ID tag read: "P. Johansson—Director of Technology."

Patrick heard the beep of the door to the lab as it opened automatically. The lab he ran held many computer stations installed upon six rows of long aluminum desks. This created a constant hum one could feel in the air. The advanced air-conditioning system made the virtual design lab one of the coldest rooms in the Complex. The heat from so many electronic devices demanded that these employees conduct their work in a mild refrigerator.

"Gentlemen," said Dr. Cotham. "Here we have one of the most advanced computer labs in the country. It would be a betrayal to not say that this is the brains of the operation."

Patrick was already walking toward the entrance to greet his guests. He noted on the way that his computer technicians had their eyes glued to their screens the entire time.

"Hello, my friends," he said jovially. "Welcome to the Architecture Laboratory. Dr. Cotham has already briefed me on what you would like to know about this magical place, so the designers and I have prepared a sample simulation for you to experience. Right this way!"

Dr. Cotham moved out of the way and gestured for the officials to follow Patrick further into the light gray lab. But before they did, Patrick heard three soft beeps. With a swift wave of Dr. Cotham's right hand at the side of her face, the tiny electronic device nestled around her ear answered the incoming phone call.

"Hello?" she answered. After a few still moments she informed her colleagues that the first patient's data file was ready to be signed off and that she would have to meet up with them later, before the next Mirage program. Patrick nodded as she left, then led his guests into the lab.

THERE WERE many places on the first floor where employees could gather to take a break and collect their thoughts. Only Madelyn chose the locker room. She had just sat down after delivering her reports to the director. The door was barely open and the lights were off. In her hands she held her phone as she slowly worked on her digital note about the events of the night, continuing with the ride on the subway and going all the way up to the first patient.

She recalled her encounter with Ms. Cross in the elevator and thought about how this would affect her placement in this institution. *The old bat is only looking for a promotion*, she thought. Then her soul began to bear a heavy weight as her thoughts gravitated back to the subway ride and her subsequent flashbacks.

The long, deep breaths that she practiced every morning for meditation interrupted the quiet of the locker room as her mind raced to find the words to describe the sensations she had felt on the train.

~

THE OFFICIALS STOOD in a group by the technical director's desk in the back of the lab. Off to the right was the door to a small, bright room with one large window.

"This room replicates the Mirage program you fellows watched on the TV monitors tonight," said Patrick. "I will explain how we extract ideas for the worlds we create after you experience it for yourself."

Beside the door to the small, bright room was a desk with a computer station, in front of which Patrick hurriedly sat down.

"So," he said as he swiveled around in the chair. "The room behind me is a test program for the real thing. It's temperature-controlled to accommodate any climate the patient wishes to experience. The floor is made of a wax substance that has, as it were, a mind of its own. It can form into any texture, replicating any terrain. It can also form into any object that is attached to the ground. Observe!" he said as he put on his reading glasses and turned to type into the computer.

Within seconds, the officials were amazed to see, through the window, the floor of the room moving like small waves. Then the white wax that made up the floor transformed into a blank outline of an antique car. The officials leaned closer to the window to see every small detail the director had programmed into the vehicle. The windows, the door handles, the interior—everything save the pure white color seemed real to the officials.

MADELYN BEGAN ADDING color to the recollections in her digital notepad—the cream of the interior of the subway car, the red velvet cover on the seats, the white lettering on the advertisements overhead, the dark blue nightfall outside that seemed to carry the subway through the city.

*Now it's all more real*, she thought.

MADELYN BEGAN ADDING color to the recollections in her

WITH ONE FINAL loud tap on his keyboard, Patrick looked through the window and then to the officials, who were still under the spell of the room before them. The exterior of the antique car turned crimson red, the wheels charcoal black, the interior creamy white. The floor around the car formed into a beautiful green landscape.

"Patrick," said one of the officials, "I see you have complete control over what people can see or touch. And it is placed together in perfect detail. But what about sound and smell?"

"I see what you are getting at, my friend. You wish to go in and see for yourself," Patrick said with a childlike smile. "Take off your shoes before we go inside, and I will show you!"

As the officials prepared to enter the digital chamber, Patrick waved to one of the architects working on a computer station nearby. Jose Pratts stood up, moved quickly to sit down at the desk by the window, and, after a few commands given by the director of technology, began typing mechanically into the computer. The room swiftly reverted to its original blank state. Patrick walked through the group of officials to the entrance. As he grabbed the doorknob, he kicked off his shoes and looked back at his companions.

"Gentlemen! Have you ever wondered what close combat in World War II was like? No matter how real this may feel to you, remember that it is all an illusion. Follow me."

MADELYN SAT in the locker room wondering about the final moments of that person in front of the subway train. Deep down within the dungeons of their mind, there must have been a great struggle between good and evil. It must have seized their whole conscience as everything else sank into insignificance. The battle must have been waged without any assistance from the outside world.

And this troubled Madelyn to the core, for her mother must have been a casualty of that same war, the war that people fought within themselves. *But perhaps good and evil don't have anything to do with it,* she thought. *In war, is it strictly a battle of morals, or is it just blood lust?*

She thought of the many times she had been faced with this question. Her hands began to shake as she jotted down notes. A battle within her began to emerge as memories came crashing in. Nostalgia was a beast ready to consume her.

THE OFFICIALS FOLLOWED Patrick into the room, and at once

they heard explosions in the distance. The room smelled of gunpowder, dirt, and exhaust fumes emitted by the virtual truck that had just driven past them. The floor developed a wet and muddy texture, and as the officials walked over it, one of them lifted their foot to see if it had stained his gray sock.

"Never mind the mud, my friend," said Patrick. "Like I said before, none of it is real! It is pure, one hundred percent virtual immersion. So feel free to walk wherever." He headed off to the side.

Outside, Jose marveled at the designs he and his colleagues were inputting into the simulation. *God, I love this part of the job*, he thought. He tapped a few more keys. The view of the window to the simulation room was interrupted by a sudden smoke or fog.

"The room is not only climate-controlled," Patrick said, "it is also scent-controlled, which means we can replicate any smell we want. The chemists on the fourth floor prepare what we need in real time. The whole building we operate in is very much alive." He paused and pointed. "Say, men, look over there!"

The officials turned their attention to the fog drifting toward them from the window. The smell of fire and smoke reached their noses.

"Do not fear suffocation," Patrick said. "It's only a simulation. Our goal here is to activate all the senses. The smell is artificial as well," he added as he walked to the center of the room. The explosions in the distance seemed to be coming nearer. Patrick stopped, turned to face the men, and, standing there in his tan suit, he raised both his hands from his side as if conducting a ceremony.

Behind him there appeared a battalion of army officers. They wore dark brown field uniforms, with wool shirts and trousers. Their olive-colored field jackets enlarged their body frames. On their faces were dirt, sweat, and an army-issued grimace, causing them to look like oddly built clones of each other. They stood at attention with rifles by their sides. This was a display the technical director had performed many times for his guests. It was his theater.

MADELYN TORTURED her mind by imagining the visions going through the person's head in those final moments on the tracks. *There must have been faces*, she thought. *Perhaps they were nameless, or perhaps they were close friends and family. Whoever they were, they too were there to wage a war.*

Her mind wandered to images of her mother lying on her bed. Injured. Spent. Weary from the long road that had brought her there. It was odd—nothing had precipitated the sudden change in her mother's demeanor. The inner battle decided to rage without cause, it seemed. Just like real wars in humanity's collective history, it could not have been predicted. Our story seemed to be war and peace.

*"Peace" was a term that became sacrilegious to mention. It was not peace that brought the person to the front of that subway train; it was the constant drums of war playing in their mind that condemned them to such a bitter end.* Madelyn wrote this stream of consciousness into her digital notes.

THE BATTALION of men stood up tall, gave a quick salute, and then ran off to the far end of the imagined field. Over a distant hill, the sun was beginning to fall as it prepared to introduce the night. Black smoke hovered on the dark horizon. The earth was muddy with patches of pale grass peppered every few feet. The ground was stamped with wheel tracks and boot prints. Gunshots rang out just behind the ears of the stunned officials. One official tricked himself into turning around to see who was shooting but was stopped when of his colleagues grabbed him by the arm and said, "Look!"

In front of them where the infantrymen were running away from the gunshots, a soldier had fallen to the ground with a painful groan. The officials ducked down in disbelief but Patrick just stood there in the middle of the field, unmoved by the sudden execution of one his creations.

"War is hell, isn't it, my friends?" said Patrick.

"This room seems so much larger than it actually is," an official marveled. "How can that be?"

"Rooms like these are designed to build the illusion not only of time and place but also, and more importantly," Patrick explained, "of space. Those far hills seem a few miles away, and we could walk there if we wish. The room would respond to how we walk, and then, with help from the artificial intelligence protocol, it would adjust accordingly."

THE AIR-CONDITIONING in the locker room sent shudders through Madelyn's body as she analyzed what she was typing. The weight of all that had happened on the evening subway ride crashed down on her—the sudden moral weight of history bearing down upon her shattered soul. Heat burst through her head as she run her hands through her hair. She focused on her breathing; the cool air seemed to dissipate.

*Just breathe*, she told herself. *Breathe, breathe...*

This was her anchor to the outside world.

JOSE GREW a mischievous grin as the simulation waged on in the room, his hands excitedly orchestrating the whole affair. And on the other side of the doors the government officials were bewildered as a sudden burst of heat took over the room.

Over the hills, brightness rose as a slight tremor grew beneath their feet. The floor began to vibrate. They looked at each other as a distant whistling reached their ears; they looked at Patrick, but he had his back to them. One of the officials suddenly bent over and made his way out the door. The remaining officials looked to the gray and black sky to see what was coming.

"Incoming!" yelled one of the infantrymen who had just run out from a trench. His panicked voice filled the room and seemed to go for eternity. The ground was seized with sudden shockwaves as the whistle turned into a piercing scream. The soldier jumped back into the yawning trench and out of their view.

The men in suits looked up in wonder as a sudden whoosh and a mighty wind stole away their vision. The whole room erupted into blackness. And everything slowly faded to gray, then to white.

MADELYN TOOK A LONG, deep breath. All at once, her anxiety withered away. The notes she had written lay on the screen of her phone like a scripture. She felt a sudden sense of peace, like the sunrise after a stormy night. It was daytime in her heart again. The war had laid down her arms, for now.

She stowed away her phone in the brown purse by her feet. Outside the dim locker room the hallway was quiet. No one else had made their way down from the upper floors for coffee break yet. Her eyes found one of the patients' letters in her purse. The emotional weight of her heart leaned against her soul. She began to formulate a plan. It involved recruiting Errol as a co-conspirator.

She placed the letter in her pocket, then made her way to the hallway that would take her to the break room. There she would wait for Errol.

**7**

———

The first-floor break room was a symphony of shoes tapping on the white-tiled floor. Employees moved to and fro. The fluorescent lights illuminated every part of the large gray room. Circular tables were placed around the center while small rectangular tables surrounded them on the perimeter. By the entrance was a beverage station with a snack bar next to it.

Madelyn stared at the dark brown sludge dripping into the foam cup. The indistinct and mumbled chattering all around her made the room somewhat lonely. She had never been a social butterfly, not even when the occasion presented itself. *My own thoughts are busy enough*, she dreamed as she poured cream into one of the two cups. In the corner of her eye she caught a familiar body moving toward her. The dark jacket with square shoulders slowly presented itself to Madelyn's full field of view.

He always carried a warm smile on his face, but not now. Now he looked anxious about something. His sapphire blue eyes betrayed the small grin he attempted to bury his anxiety with.

"Two creams, one sugar. Right?" she said.

"Yeah, that's right." Errol looked around the room and then leaned in. "Listen. I know that meeting earlier on has taken a toll on you. So if you want to end this passing of documents between us, I completely understand."

"Oh no, Errol. It's not about that. Let's find a spot where we can discuss this."

He seemed hesitant while grabbing his coffee from her hands. "Do you think this is a good place to talk?"

"I am afraid it's the *only* place. The chatter will drown us out quite nicely," she said, and smiled.

They walked through the middle of the room, past the circular tables, and settled on a square table at the far end. But before they got there, a familiar face interrupted their march.

"Listen, you two," said Jose. His eyes gleamed with excited energy. "Those government hacks just went through a war simulation, and I, the best architect this place has to offer, did us all a favor."

"What did you do now, Jose?" asked Errol. Madelyn took a sip of coffee while also taking an interest in what the officials had had to endure. Jose had been in the Complex only a few months and had already established himself as an overconfident joker.

"Mr. Johansson originally planned on a small grenade to wake up their wits, but I added in something a little more atomic. Made one of them vomit before it even hit the ground." He chuckled while swirling his coffee.

"You're lucky to have one of the most carefree directors in this place," Errol told him strictly. "Any other one would serve you papers to get you out of here."

"Something has got you in a fuss, my boy. But I get it." Jose raised his free hand to signify that he was backing off. "We're all on edge because of this damn government visit.

Just thought I would lighten the mood. How are *you* tonight, Madelyn?"

"Fantastic. But you seem to be having all the fun. If only we all had the creative freedom you enjoy!"

"Yeah. But I don't see myself sticking around after the six-month internship is over."

"Why is that?" she asked.

"I desire to build stuff that people can actually see and enjoy. Here my work gets filed away the moment it isn't useful anymore."

"Wasted art," said Errol sarcastically.

"And you'll still be here sulking over me," Jose replied. "Listen, I've got to tell the others how it went. I'll let you two get on with what you were doing." He turned and walked toward his circular table of architects.

The small talk of the employees in the large room was small indeed, Madelyn thought, compared to the weight of what she was about to discuss with Errol. They finally found their table in the corner. Slowly, as if weighted down, Errol sat down across from her. The look in his eyes was ever more interested.

At the edge of the field of people within the small break room, they engaged in inconsequential chatter. Perhaps, Madelyn hoped, it would lighten the mood. People in white lab coats surrounded the coffee machine, laughter echoed throughout the hallways, and the sound of a news report from the TV in the upper corner held some employees' attention.

In another corner of the room, attached to the wall, stood an ominous camera with a white plastic cover. The video feed from it would look like the break room of a manufacturing facility or an energy plant of some sort. From the jovial atmosphere and laid-back countenance of every person enjoying a coffee or a snack, an onlooker would never guess that this was a break room in the Complex.

Madelyn was having difficulty finding the right moment in which to broach the sensitive subject to Errol. She waited for a pause in their conversation; when it came, all the idle talk among the others in the room seemed to grow louder. This enhanced the opportunity for Madelyn to speak her mind, so she leaned in closer.

"Secrets are kept under a tight lock and key in this place," she said softly and with caution.

*This is it, whatever it is*, Errol thought. He kept his head turned slightly to the side but gazed into her inviting eyes.

"It's like we're standing on holy ground in this place, Errol. Everything is sacred, it seems." She took a sip from her coffee.

The look on her face was sincere and warm, with a way about it that could disarm an entire nation of thieves. He was under her spell.

"As it should be," she continued. "We provide the service of sweet mercy and relief for poor souls who don't have anyone or anything else. But it shouldn't be that simple. Is it?" She clasped both hands around the coffee cup. Errol slowly nodded, unable to look away.

She was whispering now. "I excel at the discovery of what drives a human being to do such things. It's a curiosity that has consumed me my entire life. But there are still missing pieces that cause me profound anguish." *Her past,* Errol thought. That sacred mystery she kept under tight lock and key.

Errol took a few sips of coffee as he pondered her last words. He felt the same way about the patients, and it was Madelyn who had helped appease that curiosity. It was a bond between them. He wondered if the other people in the break room felt the same way. Over her shoulder, he saw

Jose laughing with his colleagues, most likely telling them about his encounter with the government officials.

"Errol..." She leaned in closer to him. "All I am given access to is data and written reports from the patients. Those provide a distant sketch of who they are and what they are about." She let go of the coffee cup and reached for his hand. "The reason I have been so bothered and anxious tonight is because my heart yearns for something. The one thing I desire is to speak face to face with a patient—hopefully, tonight."

This broke the spell. Errol leaned back, let go of her hand, and took a deep breath. He looked over her shoulders again; the crowd of people seemed distant and anonymous. It was a dangerous request. But Madelyn pressed on.

"It would only be for a few minutes. I saw which Mirage room they'll be using for the third patient tonight. The only difficult thing is getting there," she said as a warm smile appeared on her face.

Her touch, her voice, her request—it all meant so much more than the consequences they would face if they were caught. *But I have to say no to this*, he thought. *It is madness, and certainly means criminal charges if the directors find out.* His mind was racing, but then a sudden thought overcame him.

"But how can you be *sure* which room they will be using?" he asked, leaning closer. "We've all heard that there may be several Mirage rooms, but it's rumor. Have *you* seen the schedule?"

"Well," she said, and took a sip of coffee, "*her* office remains open, all the time, even when she has visitors from the government. While she was out there cross-examining the departments and watching FATE in action, I dropped off the final portfolio for Patient 1258 in her office and, well, she wasn't there, so I looked through some of her files and schedules. I then gave her a phone call and left everything as it was."

"I see," he said. "You have already taken a great risk by breeching her computer. And what if we get caught doing this? Do you have an exit strategy for that?"

"I'll take the fall, Errol." Her eyes flared in intensity and resolve. "Including for the transferring of documents to you. I have a lingering feeling that Ms. Cross is already on to me. She gave me the chills this evening in the elevator." She looked over her shoulder, then turned back to him with a heartfelt invitation in her eyes that arrested all his attention. "Look," she said. "I will confess to it all as my plan only. If I could get access to speak with a patient, my soul would truly be satisfied. I just want to ask a few questions up close and personal. Then we're done."

Errol looked around to see if anyone was watching. The whole room seemed engaged in other pursuits and had no care for what Madelyn had requested of him. And this request of hers seemed to come from deep within. He looked down at their hands and then up at her. This all seemed unfair to him, but then again, was the job they were given not unfair? *Oh, how I wish I had more time to process this... What a heavy request placed upon me!* he thought. As he looked into her eyes, he imagined her giving the patient the same look of sincerity and warmth. This would somehow justify the world they were living in. *How pitiful this world is, to place two people like us in this extraordinary position!*

It became a bitter war within himself, a fight of good versus evil, but he did not know which side he was on. He resolved to buy more time from her, so he squeezed her hand and leaned in.

"I'm not saying it's impossible," he said softly, "nor am I refusing. I may need more time to gather some more information—perhaps more than a night, maybe a week. What I'm saying is, grant me the space to process all this."

"Okay. Thanks for hearing me out, Errol." Madelyn leaned back and sipped her coffee. He nodded and thought about the great lengths she had gone to provide him with letters from the patients. That was a clandestine affair they had already indulged themselves in. They both had rebel spirits, and now they were locked together in a mystery that no one knew else about.

"How does this all end, Madelyn?" he asked softly. "This institution we uphold promises a utopia of some sort."

"I suppose that *is* what they tell us. Thirty years ago, the idea of a place like this would have been complete madness."

"Yeah. Who knows what will happen thirty years from now?"

"That's supposed to be a utopia too, remember? The people on the seventh floor know all about what's best for us." She sent out a wry smile.

"History is full of those kinds of people." Errol took a drink from his coffee cup. "Sadly, the future is too. It's comforting to know that there are people willing to risk it all. I really do appreciate what you've done so far with the letters."

"Thank you. I am sorry if this request bears heavily on you. The world is upside down, and it's difficult to find any footing."

*She has a way with words*, Errol thought. "In this place of charcoal, it's conversations like these that are a spoonful of honey, Madelyn," he said. "I will try my best to find a way. I will take what you said to heart and let you know before night's end."

"Great. We should be getting ready for the next program, though," she said as she reached for the letter in her pocket.

The paper was warm and crisp in her hand. She reached under the table and tapped his leg with it. He looked down while slipping it away into his own pocket.

"Some reading material," she said. She smiled at him as she stood up, then grabbed her coffee and walked toward the exit.

Errol sat at the table by himself while a few other employees in the break room left for their departments; he was lost in his thoughts, thinking about the enormity of her request. He thought about the logistics and how they would accomplish such a feat without the authorities finding out. He thought about his friend Jose, who knew more about this building than anyone.

He thought about the letter in his pocket. He thought about the world around him.

He didn't think that he was being watched. He also didn't notice in the distance that Ms. Cross was just leaving the break room with a sinister smirk on her face, having seen all.

**8**

---

On the seventh floor, the elevator doors slid open and the government officials briskly walked out. Patrick followed them into the gray corridor. Several office doors were open as the whole building prepared for the next Mirage program. A digital clock said 12:30 a.m. as the entourage of suited men walked toward the dark office with the door slightly open.

Dr. Cotham was putting the finishing touches on a patient's portfolio when she noticed on the screen to her side a still image of Errol and Madelyn sitting across from each other in the coffee room. It was a message sent to her by Ms. Cross. The director had eyes everywhere in the institution.

The electronic devices around her reflected back to Dr. Cotham the slight grimace and wisdom on her face. She thought about the six-month internship reviews coming up and had already formed an opinion on who would be cut from the program. The small talk between the officials and Patrick finally reached the threshold to her door, and then a small knock echoed throughout the dim room.

"Yes, come in," she called out.

"Here are your guests. Safe and sound," said Patrick as he shuffled to the side of the door. The childlike grin was still painted on his face.

"Has the director of technology impressed you with all his toys?" Dr. Cotham asked the government officials.

One of the officials looked uneasy and said, "A little too much, I might say. The technology is terribly immersive."

"Cutting-edge indeed," said another.

"Used responsibly and ethically," the Dr. Cotham said, "there is no end to what we can do within the Mirage program. By the looks in your eyes, I am guessing it was the World War II simulation."

"Yes," said Patrick with a subtle laugh. "And a little fireworks display to end it off."

"Well, borderline irresponsible," she replied, "but a great take on a classic, I'm sure. Now that you have seen the literal brains of the operation," she said to the visitors, "we need be preparing for the next program. Patrick, thank you."

"Bye for now, everyone," Patrick called back as he walked off into the corridor.

"Dr. Cotham?" asked one of the men. "He mentioned that we would go over the specifics of extracting ideas for what visions appear in the Mirage program. Is there yet time?"

"We have a few minutes," she said as she grabbed a paper from the pile of portfolios next to her. "Sit down, please."

DOWN THE CORRIDOR, on the other side of the elevator doors, Patrick stood merrily tapping his left foot on the ground. He focused upward at the numbers, waiting for the ground floor to appear. When it did, the metal doors yawned open and a young man waiting for the elevator interrupted the view to the ground-floor hallway. Errol waited politely for Patrick to exit the chamber. They shared a friendly nod as Patrick walked toward the break room to grab a coffee before the next programming.

Errol stood in the elevator, pressed the number four, and waited for the metal doors to close. He stared straight ahead with his right hand in his pocket, gripping tightly onto the letter he had just read in the locker room. The distant hum and the slight clicking of the chamber moving upward provided a moment for him to think clearly. *Perhaps pressing Madelyn to allow me to read their personal letters wasn't a good idea*, he thought. *But this place has a way of pushing people; this new world has a way of pushing people.* The elevator call number skipped over the number three as he looked down at his feet. *I will give myself time to read it once more. Hopefully then I can provide an answer.*

He felt his body become lighter as the chamber slowed down and the number four appeared overheard. As the doors slid open, the corridor looked the same as it did on every other floor. He knew exactly where he would go in order to read the letter again, for he knew the ins and outs of the floor he worked on so diligently. Down near the end of the hall to the right was a fire escape that provided a blind spot from the all-seeing eye of the directors above.

He calculated the moments he had before the next Mirage program, at 1:00 a.m, and resolved to spend only a few minutes outside on the fire escape hatch. He walked lightly down the bright corridor, noticing through the wide-open glass doors his colleagues in their labs working away on their formulas and experiments. The backs of their white coats were turned to him as he looked forward to his destination.

With a quiet push of the steel door to the fire escape, he

felt the cool breeze of the night kiss his face. He looked up to see that a few clouds had appeared to block the stars from sight. The clouds offered a gloomy outlook for what he was about to do. He let the door almost shut, sat down on the steel steps, and pulled out the letter.

~

"Gentlemen," said Dr. Cotham. "It is incumbent upon every patient to provide us with handwritten letters. Most of their correspondence is catalogued by the interns, but the actual face-to-face session is conducted by the FATE program, as you have seen on the fifth floor."

With a few gestures she pulled up a holographic letter; it floated above the center of her desk. She grabbed her reading glasses with both hands and pulled them down from her white hair. The officials leaned in to see the cursive writing.

"To get a full view of the patient's mental state," the director explained, "we encourage them to write letters that are for the most part streams of consciousness. This is the last one written by Patient 1259. They are scheduled to enter the Mirage program shortly."

~

Outside on the fire escape, Errol sat holding the letter with both hands. The writing was neat and orderly. The patient had used black pen on yellow legal paper to catalogue their thoughts. It had all the elements of a love letter. He leaned in closer to protect it from the slight breeze. The forest around the Complex seemed to watch Errol prepare to read it once more. The tree leaves hushed each other as the outside lights shone down enough for him to make out the black letters on the yellow paper.

*A soul breathes freely tonight. No more talk therapy sessions with FATE, no more medication, no more cognitive behavior programs, and no more letters.*

*This body of mine has traveled the world and has seen the sorrow of a great many faces. They never seemed to look back at me, though.*

*This weathered soul that has been forged within the stormy fires of earth will finally kiss the face of a sweet infinity.*

*This soul of mine, it has traveled many leagues within itself. It has explored the greatest depths of darkness only to come up with nothing but a hope. It carries that hope while facing the path before it. My last adventure is on a road.*

*But I cannot tell if this road I am on is a path to paradise or to perdition. My soul travels alone, yet I can finally admit that there is clarity. There is freedom in this place. And because of that, I am certain there is paradise at the end.*

*I am free to take these extraordinary first steps into a land not given to suffering. It seems as if many years have passed since I first set foot in this building, and now I can walk with strength unbound away from the mental demons.*

*Bless these merciful souls within these walls, for they are the only ones who truly believed.*

*My friend FATE has told me about the control I am given in this life. For now it feels like I truly believe in the control I possess.*

*And belief has been in short supply for the entirety of my short tenure here on earth. Near the end of it all, I now bathe in the abundance of freedom and joy.*

*These days, I can truly say that I am happy.*

*My only wish is to speak to someone who has been through the same thing. Perhaps a younger version of myself, but what good would that do? What would I say?*

*In a short while, I will depart down a path of sweet escape. I cannot wait until I can gaze upon the blissful shores of my desti-nation! And I will look back one last time at the hideous path that I have traveled.*

*I will not be angry, nor will I cry. My heart will cease to shiver from the fear and suffering this world of anguish has caused.*

*As I look back I will hold my beautiful soul close to my cher-ished heart and whisper, "Thank you! And goodbye, my Dear Sweet Everything!"*

~

ONE OF THE officials pulled out a handkerchief to wipe away a tear rolling down his cheek while his colleagues looked in wonder at the final letter from the patient.

"It is awfully surreal to see the patient's last words," said the tearful official.

"It does grab the heart," said the director. "We use this correspondence to extract ideas for the virtual world which you have seen in the Technology Department." She gestured for the letter to dissolve away from the table. Then Dr. Cotham looked at the teary-eyed official in disgust. The lights grew brighter as she put away her glasses and turned her attention to the monitors. She had no patience for people who had an inclination for excess displays of emotions. To her, it was an occupational hazard.

~

ERROL FOLDED the sheet of paper and held it with both hands. He had already resolved to provide an answer to Madelyn right after the patient had finished the Mirage program. He looked up to see the clouds break. The entire night sky seemed to open itself to him, and he took a deep breath. The moon shone her gray face down through the treetops and onto the side of the building. He began thinking about what kind of virtual world the patient wished to see in their final moments. Would it be a bright moon with a sky full of stars? Or would it be beaches and blue water? *Whatever paradise they paint, I hope they find peace*, he thought as he stood up from the fire escape stairs and made his way inside.

## 9

The patient had just walked through the metal doorframe when he looked back and took one final glance at the lonely chair he had been sitting in. It stood like an iron throne. It represented his last moments breathing in the atmosphere of the bitter natural earth. On his body he wore an oversized gray suit. In his former days, he would have filled it out quite nicely. The bitter earth had stolen away his health. Underneath the suit jacket he wore a pale shirt with an aged crimson tie. It was his favorite traveling suit. It made him feel like a businessman on the hunt for a hidden treasure. It made his final quest feel much more important.

The yellow light from the Mirage room highlighted the empty throne from which he had bade farewell to the outside kingdom. Now his eyes adjusted to the sudden change in the lighting. From the dismal holding chamber to the inviting world of a promising kingdom, his thin body cast a shadow as he took a few steps into the Mirage room.

His eager, lively gaze wandered toward the button on the inside wall of the room. It stared back to him as a symbol of release and salvation. He nodded his head, then smiled as he raised his hand and pushed the button. After a click, the metal door slid closed and the window to the outside world darkened to a black abyss.

The air smelled of lavender and oak as he turned around to find the yellow fog filling the newfound environment. The mist was heavenly, and the floor felt like walking on warm soil after a gentle rain. The silence was eerie, however, until it was cut through by the distant sound of tapping. It did not sound like a clock nor did it resemble any piece of music. *Tap, tap, tap*, every few seconds. He took a few steps on the soft surface of the room.

The fog brought back memories of his travels abroad. This one time he had ascended to the top of a small mountain. At dusk he saw faint birds soaring in the distance. A pale orange horizon waved goodbye to him as the night fog took over the landscape. It was a haunting and menacing view over the lonely landscape. His thoughts would never allow him to see the beauty in it. But now, in this place, he felt true freedom.

His gray suit began to loosely ripple from a small breeze forming itself around him. His soft hand ran through his auburn hair as the world morphed into something new and exciting. The atmosphere began to change. His heart rate began a slight ascent.

As the mist dissolved, his eyes slowly adjusted to the new kind of brightness. He realized he was now standing on a concrete platform. His bare feet felt the warm touch of the gray surface. A bright and lively outdoor scene revealed itself to him. The shine of daytime stretched across the ocean-colored sky. Glancing down, he saw that the platform was an island in a sea of dirt and patches of grass; a criss-cross of steel tracks pushed away from him.

The delightful sun shone her face down while the sky swallowed up the white clouds. He felt the warmth of his face reflect the brightness back to the scenery overhead. His suit danced to the side as the clicking became louder and louder.

*Tap, tap, tap.* Then suddenly, after a gust of air and a gentle whoosh, an old vintage train appeared before him. The doors slid open in a welcoming hush. The patient looked around in amazement while perceiving his new environment in the dimly lit abandoned train station.

*This program is truly amazing*, he thought. There was no one in the terminal but him. He waited there, but the inside of the train was silent and welcoming. Looking up the track to the engine he saw steam rolling off the top, disappearing into the sky just as the clouds had. *It has been so long since an adventure has been offered to me. Anywhere but back there, please*, he thought.

He found himself stepping onto the train and looking to see that no one else was in the car. He began walking to the front of the car, feeling under his feet the vintage carpet over wooden flooring. Every step gave comfort to his legs. The fresh air lifted his spirits as he breathed deeply. Empty chairs stared back at him in the old, lonely capsule. After going through the first door and looking through the window into the next car, he felt the train suddenly begin to jerk and start moving. The tapping slowly continued its beautiful symphony.

He held onto the door handle of the next train car. The metal cooled the flesh of his hands. To the sides the landscape danced by.

The window in the door to the next train car now seemed to him like an old television screen depicting scenes from the distant past. He finally saw some life in this odd paradise.

He opened the door and crossed the threshold; the people inside took no notice of the stranger dressed in a gray suit. As the wooden door clicked into its frame behind him, he took a deep breath.

*Life, and another adventure*, he thought.

Taking a seat on the nearest bench, he took stock of the interior. Oak flooring, metal frames overhead, double-paned windows with dusty exteriors, and vibrating floors with tapping underneath. The car smelled like an ocean breeze cascading over a beach. This gave him a sense of calm and wonder; the serene atmosphere seemed to morph his body into jelly.

A man wearing a brown suit was seated directly across from him. He had his legs crossed with a newspaper shielding his upper body. The low murmur of the train rocked his body slightly from side to side. Outside, fields of green and pastures of gold passed by them. It was a beautiful mosaic of fallow and crops. *Wherever this train leads, perhaps these people will know. Then again*, he thought, *this is only a simulation, so perhaps not.*

The man across from him turned the page. The patient leaned in to see what was written above the bold headline. A sudden chill erupted up and down his spine as he read the date in black and white: June 3, 2021—the exact day he turned one. *My birthday! Well, I am thirty-one now, but these psychologists truly dig deep to find accurate treasures.*

Before he could read anything else, the man suddenly closed the paper, folded it up, and placed it to his side. He wore a brown fedora; reading glasses that hung on his stout nose. The wrinkles on his skin and neck showed that he was much further on in years than the patient. As he uncrossed his legs and sat forward, he took no notice of the man before him. The old man was nothing but a stranger traveling, but somehow his presence gave the area warmth and comfort. The old man picked up the newspaper again, stood up, and began walking toward the front of the train car.

Another person suddenly came into view. An old woman sat on a side-facing bench wearing a faded blue dress. Her dark brown hair was pulled back underneath a red cap. A pleasant smile was painted on her bright face.

One hand was resting on her lap while the other held the handle of a baby carriage. The patient leaned in closer but could not recognize the woman's face. She, too, seemed old and wise. He was suddenly distracted by the change of landscape outside as green and beige trees began to dance by them. The mosaic changed to forest scenery. Peeking through the treetops, he could dimly make out the stony peaks of mountains. *For some odd reason, this place seems familiar to me. Though I have traveled through many countries, each forest has its own identity. This one in particular*, he thought.

The train car dimmed from the lack of sunlight breaking through the trees. He took a deep breath as he watched the woman slowly move back and forth with the baby carriage. She seemed to be humming a song for her child. Along with the comforting tapping beneath the floors, her harmony created a pleasant soundtrack for his journey. This is the part of traveling he enjoyed, where one becomes nothing and the surroundings become everything.

His skin was wrapped in the heavenly atmosphere of this train car. He wondered how long this ride would be as he leaned back and stared at the lady and the carriage.

A desire to rest his eyes suddenly overcame him, but he fought it as he turned his head to the side and looked out the window. There was no one else in the train car with them so he resolved to let the ride continue without further exploration.

Suddenly, the quiet air was interrupted by three soft beeps. He turned to see the lady jump then reach for a black purse and pull out a small electronic device. A look of great sincerity and interest washed over her face as she read the message. Then she breathed deeply, began to smile, and she stood up beside her baby carriage. The wheels of the carriage turned and hummed along the wooden floor to the back of the car where the patient now stood. His eyes locked with hers in wonder.

"I had a feeling you would come," she said to him.

*Her voice is so soft and warm... and familiar. Where have I heard this before?* His mind began racing as he searched for answers. As she stood before him, his eyes stared into the windows of her soul. They were an enchanting shade of hazel, but they offered no clue as to who she was. Yet a pleasant and tender smile disarmed him.

"I have heard you traveled a great journey to get here. And from that, you must be extremely tired." She reached into the stroller and pulled out a bundle wrapped in blankets. "The path to paradise is near, but first something must be done."

The patient looked at her sideways as he began to breathe faster. His heart rate began another ascent. The scenery outside changed back to orange and golden brown fields. The sun-kissed floor lifted his mood.

"Someone wants to see you," she said as she gently handed the bundle to the patient. He leaned in close to feel the fleece blanket that wrapped the sacred treasure. The hair on his weary arms rose with anticipation of what was in the bundle. He took a deep glance into the woman's eyes. She stood back with her hand on the stroller.

"We are almost there," she said. "I will be back before then." She leaned in and kissed the patient on the forehead. The patient stared as the mysterious stranger walked softly, nearly floating, to the front of the train car. The mild click of the door signaled her exit, and he saw her body fade into oblivion, leaving him alone with the child in his arms.

The bundle moved slightly as the train sped along the track. Blurry pastures danced outside the windows. He raised one arm and began to pull away part of the white blanket underneath, his pulse beating ever so quickly. The child's arm suddenly pushed through, revealing a shocking truth that stared back at him. All at once, a tidal wave of nostalgia washed over his entire existence.

His eyes filled with tears as he placed a hand over his own mouth and he gasped. The child he was holding was himself.

The mouth, the nose, everything that *was* thirty years ago lay right here, in his weary arms.

He thought about his final letter. *Perhaps younger versions of myself, but what good would that do? What would I say?*

The train hummed its quiet song as it crawled through open fields. The patient moved rhythmically back and forth holding the small child in his arms. This impossible reunion had turned the universe inside out, and a sky full of memories flooded back into his life.

The blue-eyed baby showed laid-back composure. His fresh face never moved away from the familiar stranger before him. He seemed enchanted and amused by his much older self, the self holding onto him. And finally, as if a great spell had been broken, the patient summoned the urge to speak a kind word of welcome.

"Hello, young friend," he said, wiping away a tear from his face. The child moved his eyebrows in curiosity.

"If I could make you understand what is happening, I would. But there is not much time." He stood up and began walking around the empty car while cradling the baby in his arms.

"I guess... I..." His voice began quivering as he held onto a metal pole attached to the seats and hid his face from the child. After a few moments he regained his composure and stood up taller.

"This world—this bitter earth we grow up in—is only a moment. But I can stand here with you and say that I am truly amazed that it has happened."

A slight murmur and a twist from the baby gave acknowledgment to the patient. He had never held a baby in his arms before. The thought of becoming a father had never crossed his mind because that meant living with a family. These thoughts were catalogued in many of the talk therapy sessions he had had with FATE.

"I took great pains," he said, "to sweep away all the memories of my former life—*our* memories. This seems to be the only option for people who live in a state of emotional exile. We live in a dungeon where our memories are of no more use to us."

He looked out the window, and then held the child closer.

"There are things that will happen that are beyond your control. And I just wanted to say that I am sorry. I am so, so sorry that my heart could not turn the tide for you." He looked down; the glassy eyes stared intently back at him.

The golden brown fields danced merrily along while the sunlight kissed his skin. Brightness shone down on both of them. A holy reunion was taking place.

In the peaceful realm of the quiet train, he sat back down with the child, and they both rocked back and forth on the wooden bench. His whisper sounded distant even to himself. "I'm sorry... I'm sorry..."

Time did not exist in this new dimension. The whole universe bowed in abeyance for these kindred souls. So they sat there, looking at each other.

"Our story closes in a happily-ever-after," said the tearful patient after a while. "Perhaps there were no framed pictures of joy and love in between, but I believe it's the ending that counts the most. In a few moments, we will reach our destination and I can tell you that we will suffer no more. Happiness is just around the corner." He shuffled closer to the edge of the seat. Outside, the blurry green trees gave way to a fresh ocean view. Distant waves cascaded toward the golden shore, birds fluttered in the air, and the sky turned a beautiful purple as the horizon presented itself. It reminded him of a painting he once saw in a museum.

"I think we're here. See, look." He lifted the baby closer to his face while pointing toward the tropical blue ocean.

"There is our sweet escape."

The slight murmur of the train began to knock as the brakes squeaked. He felt his weight shift. Suddenly he heard the front door open and looked up as the lady entered with a great big smile.

"I am afraid it's time." She held her hands together in front of her. The patient acknowledged her then looked down at the child. *Those are my eyes. His existence looks so innocent and holy. The only thing I regret is leaving those glory days.*

"All right," he said, and added to the baby, "I am glad I got to see your beautiful soul one last time. There is one thing I must say before you go." He ran his finger down the child's soft face. "Through all the pain and confusion, I just want to let you know that it's all okay. After these many years, I am okay. Everything is peaceful now. *We* have found peace."

The patient leaned in and kissed his younger self on the cheek.

"Everything is okay," he whispered. "Everything is okay."

Their eyes met one final time as the patient rose and handed the child to the lady. The delicate bundle seemed to disappear in her tender arms. Thirty-one years of confusion and pain spread out before him. He stood there watching them leave while he wiped the moisture from his eyes. Thirty-one years of tears.

The train slowly ground to a halt. He took one final look back at the door through which they had faded, then opened the exit and walked out. His frail body nearly reflected the light back to the sun, he was so used to the dark. The gravel met his feet with a warm but gentle touch. The stones were soft splinters that massaged his feet.

The air smelled more strongly now of ocean tides. He stepped away from the train car and took one last glance toward the engine. The long beast gave one final hush as it began to slowly crawl away from him.

He took a step backward and bid it goodbye. He enjoyed this aspect of traveling, where one leaves and turns to the next adventure. The ocean called him. A new picture opened itself to him with a pleasing landscape. His feet felt the soft gravel turn to fine sand as he walked on.

A sudden feeling overwhelmed him. It was the idea that he was not alone, that someone had followed him. He turned and found a man next to him.

"Hello again," said the old fellow as he lifted his brown fedora. "I had a feeling in the train that you wanted to know where to go."

His voice was coarse and bore evidence of many years of wisdom. He stood at the same height as the patient and regarded him with wonder and curiosity.

"Yes." The patient cleared his throat. "I have been wondering where this all leads to. Somewhere far from here, I suppose."

"Well, you need not worry, young man. There are places beyond the ocean that you haven't yet seen. Places not given to suffering."

"For thirty-one seasons I have hoped for such a place.

Maybe now, it is near." The ocean breeze swept through him. "I have seen people in this vision who I do not recall meeting in that other hideous world. Tell me, old friend. Where have I met you before, if I ever have?"

The old fellow smiled and his eyes narrowed as he stepped closer to the patient. "You have met me before. All your life you have been meeting me, day after day."

Seagulls began to cry out in the distance as gentle waves crashed onto the beach. Small shrubs and foliage spoke of the gentle breeze that caressed them. All of nature seemed to welcome the men there.

"But that is enough for now," the old man said. "We must be going, my dear friend." He lowered his head and gestured toward the beach. The patient turned to see a wooden dock in the distance. At the end of it bobbled a white boat with two sails cracking in the wind. "Paradise awaits. I will be your guide."

They began their holy march along the golden beach. The patient turned to look at the old man; he was smiling as he walked ahead. There was a certain grace in his steps. The patient felt at home in this alien world. There was no threatening atmosphere where they walked. The wide ocean spread out over the horizon as they reached the dock. Small waves crawled up the beach and toward their feet. The refreshing wind pushed itself into his lungs as he breathed deeply.

*Life*, he thought.

As they approached the shore end of the dock, he took notice of the sailboat's modest size. It had white siding with two benches attached to its wooden frame. He had a few faded memories of sailing, but he tried hard to suppress even those that appeared in this dream world.

The water gently pushed up against the wooden legs of the dock as the men marched forward. The hard, cool platform turned the patient's feet into firm electrodes. He was slowly regaining his traveling legs after the unnatural floor of the Complex. Every step felt electric. *Walking with strength unbound*, he thought.

They reached the end of the dock. The old man took off his brown jacket to reveal a white dress shirt. He gestured for the patient to enter the boat. "After you, my friend." His withered hand reached out to assist his younger friend into the boat.

The old fellow's firm grip reminded the patient of someone, but he could not figure out who. The cool floor of the boat kissed his feet as he shifted his weight along with it. He turned around to watch the old man untying the knots. The youthful vigor in his movements began to enchant the patient.

"Well, there's not much on land for us anymore," the old fellow said merrily, "but across this water—a sweet escape."

His radiant face and jovial voice seemed to echo through the air as he jumped into the boat. After setting the sails and putting the ropes away, they stood side by side as the distance between them and the dock began to grow. The patient looked toward the green and golden land. With a long, wholesome sigh, he placed his hand on the old fellow's shoulder and said, "Yes. A sweet escape."

Once they were further out to sea, and after the patient had run his hand along the water many times, he looked back once more to the land and stood up. His legs were strong and firm. The breeze had risen to a temperate wind and his gray suit moved quickly along with it. He gently removed his jacket and tucked it underneath the middle bench.

The sails cracked along with the moving seascape. The old fellow, holding onto the rudder, regarded him standing there.

The intense glow of the sun lit up the atmosphere, and the patient did not feel a deep and longing pain in his heart anymore. A sudden wave of euphoria swept over him, and he cried. He cried for all the years he had wandered through the dark world behind him. He cried for those still lost in the wilderness. And he cried tears of joy and happiness.

He waved a hand in the air as he wiped his tears away with the other. "Goodbye," he whispered, "my Dear Sweet Everything."

The distant shoreline began to fade into a bright abyss. The blue waves dissolved into the horizon in every direction. There was a great peace to this environment. There was a sense of harmony and balance in the air. He looked around and then to the old fellow.

"We are not far from our destination," the old man said. "But first, you must rest, my friend." He gestured behind the patient.

Near the bow of the boat there appeared a soft mattress with blankets and pillows. It looked awfully inviting, and the patient began to feel dreary and tired. A lonely tear ran down his cheek as he smiled and walked to the front. His sea legs had finally, fully returned to him.

*In another life, perhaps I was a famous sailor or explorer*, he thought.

The water gushed and hushed against the sides of the wooden boat. A few birds cackled in the distance.

The patient lay down on his side. The mattress was comforting and delightful, like an oasis within another oasis. The old fellow moved to the middle of the vessel. He took his place and sat there; his white hair stirred along with the wind. The laugh lines on his face revealed a life of joy tempered by hardship.

"We made it," he said softly. "We are going where the beautiful souls go. Both yours and mine."

The patient felt another warm tear crawl down his face. He looked deeply into the old man's eyes. And he realized he was looking into his own. He was looking into a mirror of his own soul.

"We are going home," the patient whispered.

His gaze wandered up toward the heavens. His eyelids slowly began to close. His body began to feel weightless as he felt happiness and infinite joy descend upon him. A new world was opening itself up to him. With his eyes closed and his hands clasped together on his chest, he took one final, peaceful breath.

The ocean water ceased to crash against the boat as it became still as ice. The sails stopped cracking as the winds hushed and dissolved into nonexistence. The sun sang her final song and set on the world that surrounded him.

**10**

———

The entire Complex seemed to expand and deflate in a relieving sigh, as one sighs when a stressful situation has passed. Every intern, permanent employee, security guard, director, doctor, scientist, and visiting member felt a huge weight lift off the rooftop of the institution they were contributing to. They breathed more easily in a unifying symbol that, somewhere in the building, a person had found freedom.

Or at least that was the feeling in the seventh-floor office. Dr. Cotham glanced at the digital clock on the dark wall. She wrote down "2:05 a.m." in the patient's file as her dark hazel eyes found the officials closely huddled around the TV monitor. On the screen they saw a group of men in decontamination suits crouched over a lifeless body. Patient 1259 lay on the wax flooring with his arms crossed over his chest. A slight zoom of the camera lens brought into view a peaceful smile below closed eyelids. Dr. Cotham's eyes shone in response.

"But where does the body go after the program is done?" asked one of the officials.

"Part of the Mirage program is granting the patient full control over what happens to their body," the director replied. "Some desire cremation, some a burial, but most wish to donate themselves to science." The corner of her mouth smiled as she looked at the monitor. "This man specifically, he wanted a cremation. Our facility is not a funeral home, so the body is escorted offsite, into the city."

All four sets of eyes stared at the doctors on the TV monitor. One doctor, holding a clipboard, was writing down vitals while the other two lifted the patient onto a stretcher.

"Has FATE ever convinced a patient to not go through with the Mirage program?" the official, who earlier had shed a tear, inquired.

"When we started designing the program, it was agreed by all parties that the principal idea of FATE was data collection," Dr. Cotham offered while staring into the TV monitor at the young man. "FATE was never meant to intervene in the inevitable but rather to provide a rational choice for the patient to make. And all of the time, one hundred percent of the time, the patient has chosen to find release and salvation through the Mirage program. Once again, the patients believe more in the program than we do."

It took a few moments for the officials to grasp the weight of her answer, but after some personal introspection they began to realize that what the Complex provided was mercy and justice. These were in short supply in that age; within those walls, the top-level administrators were deeply faithful to the principles of FATE.

"Has there ever been an instance," an official asked, "where the chemicals were not lethal enough for the patient?"

"Heavens, no," the director snapped. "There has not been one case of malpractice at our facility. The chemists we employ are world class and fully aware of the consequences if a program fails one of the patients. They take painful steps to carefully analyze all the data before them." She stood up and walked toward the door. "I will take you to the fourth-floor labs to see for yourself. Follow me."

The ambitious group of pioneers moved out into the bright hallway and then along to the elevator that would take them to see the chemistry lab firsthand. Back in Dr. Cotham's office, the TV monitor displayed the doctors zipping the deceased patient into a black body bag. As they wheeled the patient off the premises, the large, ominous Mirage room began to dim.

IN THE INTERNS' lab, Errol was startled by the sudden beeps coming from the loudspeakers overhead. The Mirage program had just completed and the doctors had escorted the patient's body offsite. This was the cue to scrutinize the data and prepare their final reports. He was still not use to this moment. *I don't know if those beeps will ever sound dull to me. This place feels new every day*, he thought as he gripped the patient's letter in his pocket. Behind him, a group of men and women in lab coats were discussing how the patient had responded to the aromatic chemicals from the ocean air.

"The director said this was the best one yet," one scientist said. "The seawater replication brought the patient to near nirvana, the report says!"

*They gush, but their voices sound dull to me*, Errol thought. *The way they celebrate is near morbid. Everybody's sounding too much like Jose.* He grabbed a few empty charts to begin his version of the program.

But the entrance door to the lab slid open. The click echoed around the room as all eyes turned to the door. Dr. Cotham and her esteemed guests walked in.

"And here we have the main chemistry lab, gentlemen. I guess you could say that this is the *nose* of the operation," she added wittily.

The director on this floor was a short, bald man who rarely left his desk at the back of the room. His face always looked weary but his eyes were full of life. He was a famous recluse in the Complex, not known for any social interactions beyond his official duties—a very serious man, but the best in his field. Underneath his lab coat was a tag that read: "H. Albright, Director of Science."

Henry looked over at the approaching group with a great deal of concern in his eyes. Errol knew him to be a very gentle human being but socially awkward. Granted, he also knew that the old man would have rehearsed the speech beforehand in order to avoid any embarrassment.

"Over here," the director said, "is the greatest scientist of all time: Henry Albright." She firmly shook his hand and her devoted followers did the same.

"Thank you for the kind introduction," Henry stated mechanically.

After all the necessary formalities were complete, the lab fell into an awkward silence. Dr. Cotham then turned to all the onlookers and waved them on. "Do not mind us everyone. Please go back to work."

Errol turned back to his desk; the theater of senior leadership had unfolded. His thoughts wandered to the letter in his pocket while he busied himself with generating reports.

"Well," the director of science said. "I guess I should show you around. Our principal concern down here is health and safety, so if you could wear these goggles and coats, that would be brilliant. We can begin at the holo-graphic computer, if that suits you, Doctor?"

"Yes, please lead the way," the director replied.

"In this lab," Henry explained, "we have thirteen certi-fied staff members and three interns who help us during and after programming. This is so..." His voice trailed off away from Dr. Cotham as he strolled to the center of the room with the officials following. Instead the director wandered the lab, analyzing the work being done by the scientists.

Henry stopped by a chart on the wall near her. He began to explain how they calculated the right mixture of chemi-cals needed to place the patient "under a spell." He pointed to a formula that helped explain the relationship between the size of the room, the size of the patient, and exactly what amount of nitrogen was employed to place the patient into a deep, euphoric sleep.

But Dr. Cotham had caught a side glimpse of Errol from the other side of the laboratory. She immediately recognized him from the footage with Madelyn. Like a predator seeking its prey, she carefully approached the unsuspecting intern. He was fidgeting with something in his lap—something clandestine, it seemed.

The cool lab air was full of chatter and keyboard typing; he would never hear her soft steps. Within a close earshot she made herself known.

"Excuse me," she snapped. Errol jumped in his seat. The men continued chattering across the lab; a few scientists glanced toward the sudden interrogation unfolding in the corner.

"The Mirage program has just ended," the director declared, "the government officials are in the room, and here you are appearing to waste precious time. What exactly were you doing?" She was now a defense lawyer cross-examining a witness.

"I didn't mean to offend anyone, Doctor," Errol said apologetically as he turned around to face her, "but this particular formula needed to be done with a calculator." He held up the electronic implement with a look of regret.

The surrounding scientists returned to their work, but Errol was sure they were still eavesdropping. The buzz of the air conditioning and the tap-tap of typing echoed through the bright lab.

"You have been a junior chemist for four months now, is that correct?" the director asked. Errol nodded with a smile he hoped did not show his nervousness.

"Then you should know," Dr. Cotham admonished, "that everything is being watched within these walls. A junior staffer staring down into a device on his lap looks suspicious to anyone analyzing the feed. Be more careful and more transparent about your activities. Remember that in this place, there is *always* someone watching."

Errol knew that the only places without cameras were the fire escape and the holding chamber before the patient entered the Mirage room. But that was not the only intelligence he had about this grave institution. He had spent many nights at a downtown bar while Jose spilled secrets about this place. Jose's rebellious nature outweighed the constitution of the Complex. He was both brilliant and stupid.

"Yes, ma'am," Errol replied. "In the future I will be more transparent with my calculations. I do apologize."

"And one more thing." She leaned in and said, in a low, sinister voice, "A chemist has no business polluting the mind of a psychologist. Ms. Cross, who you know about from the meeting this evening, is close to finding out who the detractors are in this place. My advice to you is to leave the other interns alone. When your six-month term is over, do not expect an extension of employment."

Errol glanced at the ground, trying to find an answer to her threat. But when he looked up, the menacing glare of the director's eyes stared back at him. There was a certain kind of evil hidden behind those eyes. It was an evil dark enough to blind the soul of someone whose job it was to assist the death of so many people in this odd institution.

Errol had begun to see a different side of the patients by reading their letters, all thanks to Madelyn taking a huge risk. This sudden ill treatment by the director strengthened his resolve. After the reports were done, he would arrange for Madelyn to speak with one of the patients. But first he would send a message off to his other comrade regarding this new development.

~

"SHE WANTS TO DO *WHAT*?" Jose asked uneasily.

"All she needs is a few minutes," Errol explained. "Look, we have confirmation that the third patient will be in the Mirage room directly below me, so all we need is a dust-up." A glint of moonlight reflected off the nearby windows. The dark trees rustled a soft song as the two of them faced each other on the fire escape.

"But if the interview fails and we get caught, you know that it could be criminal charges, right, Errol? You know what we signed up for."

"I know. Any sign of dissent is punishable by law, according to the tyrants on the seventh floor."

"This is not dissent, this is... destruction." Jose shuffled away from him and leaned over the metal railing, staring into the black abyss of night.

"Our entire society bathes in destruction," answered Errol.

"You know," Jose replied solemnly, "I wonder about this odd institution and its place in society. It may seem like I am having all the fun in the world, but the truth is, I struggle to believe."

Errol noticed Jose's gaze wander down and away from the dark of night. He was indeed looking for answers somewhere beneath him.

"You're not alone in the struggle, my friend." He placed a soft hand on Jose's shoulder. "A great darkness has charmed a lot of us into thinking there's no hope, but trust me. Look up there—you will see."

At once the clouds broke, revealing a bright vista full of stars and galaxies. Jose's eyes found their way upward, and shone in response. After marveling for a few moments, a thought overcame him.

"Somewhere up there, in another planet in another galaxy, perhaps someone has it all figured out. It kind of makes the job worth it, knowing that there's a truth out there. But still, some days are tough, man." Jose gazed down again and sighed deeply.

Errol smiled warmly at his friend. "What we do here, beneath the shadow of doubt," he said, "it's not all for nothing. There's a reason we're here, and a reason you and I are in this struggle."

"That part can be true," replied Jose. "But tell me, when you were going through it, what kept you going? What made you put one foot in front of the other?"

Errol's mind began to wade through the waves of memories that flooded his soul. Flashbacks pushed back against him, visions of his brother and how empty his eyes were in those last dreadful days. If the life of his brother were a flower, then he witnessed it slowly wilt until, one by one, its petals slowly dropped and faded into oblivion. In the garden of life, another flower had passed too soon.

Fifteen years ago, it had seemed that the whole earth had been gasping for air. A spiritual plague swept through the nation, leaving a trail of bodies in its wake. The world never seemed to have recovered from this dark age.

In those days, he had felt it happening to him gradually, like a cosmic vacuum patiently sucking the life right out of him. He initially attributed this feeling to mere circumstance or to a society in chaos, but now these reasons only seemed to touch the surface of a much larger ocean of despair. So he took a dive to see what was beneath. And after a few more still moments, he found the words to describe what it had been like.

"Everything seemed to be crumbling down—I mean the structures all around us. And that led me to question if all our mental anguish reflects society's ills. Or perhaps it's the other way around." Errol looked up, and to Jose it seemed he was marveling at the stars above. "See, when after a few days we found his body, the authorities never gave us a chance to search for answers. I guess it was their policy of erasing deaths like this from the history books. So if a major institution doesn't value a life like that, then how are we to value our own? We become disposable, recyclable, to the systems that were meant to protect us."

Jose nodded. In their few months working alongside each other, it had been refreshing to share deeply held personal views. He regarded these as sacred, and much better than the standardized counseling sessions they were all required to undergo with FATE. He hung onto every word of his friend's confession.

"But then," Errol continued, "I thought about the inverse, and how personal anguish could be the root of it all. This is where I got lost. This is where I realized that it's not about shifting blame, which is what I got caught up in. This is about finding the origin story of a sickness, a trauma, a spiritual mourning. And I fell into a dark, deep pit, never leaving my bed for days on end. It was a fight every day just to open my eyes, because when we're asleep, we don't feel anything. And that was my only escape.

"But then I went through a transformation, and I began to wonder how to salvage anything from the rubble all around me. Even if the social structures don't value the lives of their people, there has to be another way. So I resolved to avenge someone's death, in a way." Errol's eyes seemed to gloss over the unfortunate situation they were all placed in. "I resolved to find truth no matter the cost. Even if it means descending into a deep depression, even if it means trying to find answers in a hopeless place, even if it means enlisting myself to assist the government in operating one of their cherished institutions. Call it a fool's errand, but at least it's a meaningful pursuit, with a purpose. At least that's what I think."

A few gray clouds stretched across the sky, blotting out the view of the moon and the stars, like curtains closing on the personal monologue of someone who dared to dream about truth.

"Well," replied Jose, "if being a scientist doesn't work out here, you can always be hired as a therapist. That was extremely intriguing and thoughtful, man."

Their laughter echoed through the surrounding forest.

"Dear god," Jose said. "That was way better than those responses we get from FATE. I swear that AI is misguided. No compassion, all intellect. But I hear you." Jose placed a hand on Errol's shoulder. "We've all been placed in an extraordinary position where our own morals are brought into question. And your response was valid—it brought a new angle in to look at it from."

They stared ahead together beyond the woods, finding the orange haze that hovered above the city—comrades sharing a private exchange during a pause in the great war waged within.

Jose broke the silence. "I heard they're clearing away the industry ponds on the west side for another Complex. One of the senior architects told me over coffee."

"They used to farm fish over there, right?"

"Yeah... my uncle used to ship them supplies from the docks. Apparently the entire area will be closed off soon. Just like this one."

"They used to make life over there," Errol quietly declared.

"I guess that depends on which angle you look at it from," said Jose. "If you would have told me fifteen years ago that life would be like this, I would have thought that somehow we could turn it around. But no, here we are. Assisted suicide facilities abound."

"What about fifteen years from now?" asked Errol. His curious gaze wandered toward his friend.

"Truthfully? This will all be like a fast food franchise, a Complex popping up in every city. People lined up out the door." Jose outstretched his arms to illustrate his point.

"God, I hope not... But then again, look where we are."

"No matter how you put it, none of it really makes sense. I'm starting think that it's designed that way," said Jose sardonically.

"Well, you have a taste for good design. What other way would you have it?" Errol inquired.

"Less authority with more independent thought. This is coming from someone with no authority, though."

"Some of the best thoughts usually do." Errol reached for his pocket and grabbed the letter. The clouds seemed to gather, causing a darker atmosphere as he handed it to him.

Jose took it. "What's this?"

"Madelyn pulled it from a patient's files tonight. We've been sharing their letters for some time now." Errol stared his friend down. The leaves whispered as a breeze danced through the air and onto the fire escape where they stood.

Jose glared down at the folded paper in his hand. He seemed paralyzed. Errol thought back to the standoff between his own heart and mind. He had wanted deeply to understand the thoughts of what the patients were going through, but he also wanted distance between himself and their battle. He wondered if Jose was the same.

"So this is what the fuss was about in the meeting," Jose said animatedly. He shook the paper at Errol with a condescending smirk. "You two keep your secrets to yourselves. But I understand. You've fully invested yourself in this plan already."

"You're not the only one with secrets about this place, Jose," Errol replied.

"I guess not."

"So what can you tell us about the third floor?"

"I have access to Johansson's security key. I can enable the third-floor fire escape doors so she can get in. I suppose I can jam Dr. Cotham's computer feed to prevent them watching it all, too."

"You can actually do that?"

"She said herself that we're the brains of the operation. You're looking at them." Jose pointed to himself in a fit of prideful arrogance. In his mind, Errol realized, he *was* the authority figure.

"It's great," Errol said, "to see that there's some vanity left in this world."

Jose handed him the letter but playfully pulled it away before Errol could grab it.

"And make sure it's worth it. She'd better walk away

from this interview with the answer to all life's questions, the existence of God, or a cure for all society's ills." He handed the letter to Errol. "Please."

"We will find some truth out of all this, I promise." Errol followed Jose back into the gloomy building, leaving behind the cosmos towering above the bitter earth.

**11**

———

Distant footsteps echoed throughout the dismal air on the first floor. Faint voices from the coffee room danced through the atmosphere. The clock hanging at the end of the corridor said 2:30 a.m., one hour until the last patient would undergo programming. In the locker room, she sat with her head in her hands. The lights were off. She breathed deeply while listening to the sounds of the busy institution around her. None of the other employees spent time in the locker rooms until the end of the night. This was her sanctuary. It was a place where she could gather all her strength. The locker room was an island in an ocean of despair.

She reached into the purse to pull out her phone. There were a few mental notes she wanted to write down. *Hopefully, Errol has made a decision. I don't blame him for taking the time. This hideous place wears down one's soul quickly,* she thought.

The notes she opened up were a series of questions she had been preparing over the months here. She had experience with interviewing patients from her past work in several clinics throughout the city, but she had never talked to someone whose life would be over within an hour, so this interview would be remarkably different. Her phone vibrated and a message appeared on the front screen.

*Thought this would be much safer than in person. The plan is a go for tonight.*

Her heart skipped a few beats as she felt the weight of the room lift. The sun shone brighter over her island.

*Thank you so much, Errol!*

She waited for the particulars to be sent back to her. The anticipation began to lean on her conscience. It was certainly a novel experience, being part of a clandestine affair.

*A friend in the Technology Department has agreed to disable surveillance features to prevent us from detection. At 3:15, go down the fire escape to the fourth floor. I will meet you there to give you an earpiece so we can communicate.*

His message was like an ocean vessel sent to save her from the desolate island she'd been resigned to.

*Absolutely. Can't wait to see you.*

They resolved to delete the conversation for an extra-safe measure. Within those walls, nothing, it seemed, stayed private.

Madelyn was thrilled to see that the plan would finally hatch. The notes she had been building up were meant for what would happen within the next hour. A time and place had been set. Yet the unease was overwhelming. Her mind began to race as she searched for long breaths to help anchor the outside world. But before she could, the lights flipped on, followed by a loud thud.

"Madelyn," said a familiar high-pitched voice.

She turned around to find Edith leaning into the locker-room door. "Dr. Cotham wishes to speak with you, before the next programming. She says it is rather urgent."

*Dammit. She must have seen us in the break room, or*

*perhaps someone was eavesdropping. I bet it was grumpy old Ms. Cross.* Her face grew flush with nervousness at the idea of facing authority when she had such rebellious plans for the night. Her hands were gripped tight together like handcuffs, like a prisoner destined for their sentencing. *Deep breaths... Act natural...*

"Yes, of course," she said out loud. "I'll be there right away."

A million hideous thoughts ran through her mind as she stood up, walked out of the locker room, and nodded to her younger colleague, who seemed ill at ease from some prior encounter. Fear seized Madelyn's body. The island she had built had dissolved in front of her very eyes.

THE SEVENTH-FLOOR HALLWAY WAS EMPTY. Slight tapping noises and distant murmurs traveled through the air. Near the end of the hallway, opposite the elevator, a door was nearly closed. Behind it the director lay back in her chair with her hands behind her head. Her gaze was fixed on a TV monitor. On the screen were several scenes of Complex employees preparing themselves to navigate the last few hours of the night. Her sinister eyes watched the fourth-floor lab technicians scurry to and fro, Errol typing away on his keyboard, Henry Albright glaring at some charts in front of him. She saw Jose among the sea of architects working away in a lab full of computers.

And she saw Ms. Cross on her digital monitor diligently cataloguing records and filing them. Her domain was on the second floor, where employees seldom visited. It was only Ms. Cross and a digital librarian who ruled the second floor. Not much was said about what happened on that floor other than by a few interns who believed Ms. Cross was an evil witch hell-bent on getting everyone in trouble. She had a ruthless reputation. Everyone in the Complex had heard whispers about her, but nothing was certain.

Dr. Cotham heard a noise outside her office and pushed a button on her desk. All the monitors turned off. The office lights grew brighter.

Madelyn took a deep breath and leaned in while softly knocking. "Hello? You wanted to see me?" She had cleared her throat several times in the elevator while dressing up an alibi that would clear both her and Errol.

"Please, come in. Shut the door behind you." It was rare for the door to her dark chamber to be closed.

Dr. Cotham stood up and leaned forward with hands spread on her desk. Her gaze was focused on the pile of papers on her desk. Her stance portrayed her as a powerful mistress over her dominion. The office around her echoed the power she wielded.

Madelyn remained quiet while delicately closing the door. The click echoed through the large office. It seemed like a long walk until she finally reached the chair and sat down. Her legs were crossed. Hands were on her lap. And she sat up straight to face the music.

Dr. Cotham responded by sitting down and leaning back into her large black chair. *Her throne*, Madelyn thought. After a few moments, the director reached for the pile of papers and pulled out a dark blue portfolio. She placed it in the center of the dark table. The blood in Madelyn's body seemed to rush from all of her limbs to her head.

"As you have heard a thousand times since you started four months ago, you know about the sensitive nature of our work. Confidentiality is king, but we also demand a strict code of transparency from people who are given access to certain information." The director's dark hazel eyes glared at Madelyn.

The young psychologist took deep breaths and began to feel the sweat forming on the top of her forehead. The TV monitors behind Dr. Cotham gave the impression that she was listening to a silhouette. Madelyn nodded in agreement.

"We are a relatively young program with a promising future." Dr. Cotham stood up and wandered over to one side of the office. With one graceful movement, she pulled her reading glasses down from her white hair. She began to read a few charts on the wall and pointed to a number. "The first patient finished the Mirage program in June of 2048. Ten years before that, an idea had emerged from a group of psychologists, digital architects, and computer engineers. They wanted to be on the cutting edge of artificial intelligence by creating a program that would be able to conduct therapy sessions. They wanted to be on the frontier, so they created FATE. They also wanted to create ideal virtual worlds extracted from the thought patterns of suicidal patients." Her finger slid forward to another number.

"After five years, along with improvements in artificial intelligence, advanced therapy was born and was deployed in trial sessions. FATE surpassed all of our best psychologists. And along with it, the virtual worlds were perfected even beyond our wildest dreams. Knock-offs of our first-generation Mirage rooms proliferated around the country. People needed to escape."

Madelyn stared at the chart in wonder. A detailed timeline of how the Complex came to be! Its history had been briefly outlined to her before she started employment, but not in such detail, and not from one of the masterminds herself.

Dr. Cotham sighed deeply then turned around and walked to the side of her desk. She picked up the dark blue portfolio and began searching for something. A glint from the faint hallway light coming in under the door reflected off her glasses. Madelyn felt her clenched hands begin to numb. *She's making quite the show of this interrogation.* Was she stalling so that the plan would be foiled? *This whole sermon seems rather odd*, she thought.

After crawling over several pages with two fingers, the director finally found what she was looking for. Her eyes met Madelyn's for what seemed to be the first time in the meeting. She slid out a thick sheet of photograph paper and gently laid it in front of her. The deafening silence caused Madelyn's heart to race faster as she leaned in to see.

"Tell me." The director turned around and slowly walked away. "Have you ever heard the name Elizabeth Baldwin?"

It was a black and white photograph of a young lady lying on top of a crushed antique car. Her bare feet were crossed. She was wearing what looked like a 1950s swing dress. One arm lay across her chest and the other hung off to the side. The hand on her chest firmly gripped a chain with a shiny locket. The calm demeanor of her face portrayed a sleeping beauty. But the car's folded roof and broken glass portrayed a person swept from the earth much too soon.

Madelyn gently picked up the photo and shook her head.

"That photo," the director said, "was taken on June the thirtieth, 1949, by an amateur photographer who happened to be standing by. Not much is known about Elizabeth in her final hours, or much about her life, to be honest." She grabbed her coffee mug and walked behind the desk toward the other wall.

"They found her handwritten note and jacket on the top floor of Petersburg Clock Tower. Remarkably, she cleared the setbacks after jumping down from over seventy-three stories. In her note she requested to be cremated and never to be remembered again." She turned and stood staring into oblivion across the dim office.

Madelyn felt sweat crawl down the side of her neck. Her eyes were fixated on the dreamy state Elizabeth seemed to be forever engraved in. It looked as if she was sleeping and waiting to be awoken. She looked peaceful. Her one hand, barely clenched onto the locket, made the whole scene mysterious and haunting.

At once an image of her mother came crashing in like a wave. The sepia photo in Madelyn's purse portrayed her mother with the rarest thing she ever possessed, her smile. Ever since Madelyn could remember, that smile had been strong enough to calm the threatening existential storms of life. Near the end of her mother's life it had been rarer than the world's most precious diamond.

"Little did she know," the director now said, "that this photo would make its way into every major publication around the world. Back then it was part of the culture to put these on the front page. Everyone across the entire world saw it. And it would be called 'The Most Beautiful Suicide.'"

Dr. Cotham sighed deeply once again and looked down at her feet.

"You see, Madelyn," she continued, "I am sure you have contemplated the philosophy behind what we do here at the Complex. It has probably haunted and vexed you to think about it."

Madelyn placed the photo back on the desk. Who in their right minds *wouldn't* contemplate it? It was only human to do so.

"We all," Dr. Cotham confessed, "become devoured by the question of why. Sometimes I find *myself* lost in thought about it. But you know"—she set down her coffee mug, took a seat, and leaned back—"a society premised on freedom and liberty is a truly noble thing, or so they say. I grapple with what is truly noble on a daily basis. And I am one hundred percent certain that Elizabeth grappled with this also."

Dr. Cotham grabbed the photograph from in front of Madelyn and began to admire the picturesque young lady.

"In her world, that was the greatest struggle. It was her own personal world war."

Madelyn felt her body relax and her heart rate began its descent. It was mesmerizing to watch the director at her most vulnerable. The woman almost had an attraction to the young lady in the photograph.

"And it is of the utmost importance," Dr. Cotham said, "that she was given the right to fight that war within herself. She had the freedom to do it. She was given full dominion over what her life would become." Her regard wandered toward Madelyn. "That is what the Mirage program is for, Madelyn. For patients who feel as if they have lost their locus of control, we return it to them through advanced therapy and dream-world release. Secondary objectives are to understand the problem much better than we use to. But primarily"—she stood up again—"we are here to facilitate people's freedom of choice. And if their choice is to leave in the same spirit as Elizabeth did, then we want to ensure that they, too, are given the most beautiful suicide."

The photo in her hands began to lower as she stared at it. Her hand gently caressed the surface as Madelyn watched her worship it. The ruler over her own dominion must have her personal gods. Moments became hours as Dr. Cotham finally moved her gaze away.

"Of course, with any pioneering efforts there is always resistance." The photo was forcefully dropped onto the desk. Dr. Cotham crossed her arms while glaring at Madelyn. "What happens in the minds of the patients, their interviews, their thoughts, their dreams—all of this is strictly confidential. And I am getting the feeling that some people do not understand that." She stood still as a statue.

Madelyn's heart rate began its ascent once again. "Dr. Cotham, I—"

"Please." The director lifted a hand then placed it on her own forehead. "There are questions that need answers, Madelyn. There are leaks in this organization that threaten the overarching goals of this place. I am sure you remember our meeting this morning."

Sweaty palms. Dry lips. Her body was locked in place and she did not know where to go if she *could* go. Like a prisoner awaiting her sentencing, she prepared to feel the worst blow to her soul.

A low ringing noise began to form in the back of her mind. Madelyn looked down at her lap and felt the entire world collapse beneath her feet. Suddenly, she felt a warm touch on her right shoulder. She looked up to see that it belonged to Dr. Cotham. A warm smile appeared on the director's face as she leaned in.

"And I know that you can help me find them."

Madelyn felt a deep sigh emerge from her own soul. The world formed itself around her again. The dark abyss dissolved as her island began to feel palpable once more. She could breathe again.

"Everybody trusts you, Madelyn. There is a certain amount of confidence people have in you. Certainly, your peers do." Her hand left the shoulder as she made her way back behind the desk.

"This is unprecedented in my time as director. But with your sparkling reviews from the clinics you worked at, with the esteemed research papers you produced in college, and with our own internal assessment of how you handle the portfolios of every patient, I want to offer you permanent employment as assistant director of your department." Dr. Cotham's smile grew ever larger as she leaned forward on the desk. The subtle office lighting seemed to illuminate the world around the two of them.

Madelyn let out a few short gusts of breath. Her hands relaxed. Her eyes moved toward Dr. Cotham's as she stood up taller in her chair. *So that's what this intricate sermon was about. She doesn't know! But perhaps she's playing on a multi-level chessboard. It would be foolish to refuse.*

"What do you think of this offer?" the director asked.

"Yes. Um, of course. I accept the position." She tried to say it with the most enthusiasm she could muster.

"Fantastic. With greater responsibility, you can narrow in on the supposed leaks we have within the Complex," Dr. Cotham said with an air of relief. "You know, the government officials were impressed by the way you carried yourself earlier. You're one of the greatest minds we have. The transition to senior staffer will take a few weeks, but you will find your feet quickly, I assume." Dr. Cotham stood up and reached out for a handshake.

Madelyn woke up from her daze. The hideous spell was broken. Her rapidly moving thoughts were still processing the weight of it all. *I thought for sure it was over.* After wiping the sweat off her hand, she shook Dr. Cotham's.

"It's almost three," Dr. Cotham said, "so we had better get ready for the last Mirage program of the night. Thank you, Madelyn."

"You are welcome. I look forward to it."

The black and white photo of Elizabeth Baldwin stared back at her while she stole one final glance at it. The woman's body looked carefully placed on a bed full of horrors. The young woman holding the locket looked so peaceful. Her face was calm and gentle. *It really does look beautiful*, she thought.

Dr. Cotham watched her star pupil walk down the hallway toward the elevators, then she went back into her office to see where the officials were. Everyone in the Complex was preparing for the last patient of the night.

## 12

The time was 3:00 a.m. when Madelyn sat down back in her quiet island on the ground floor. Fifteen minutes to spare until her interview with patient number three. She tried to shake herself off of the rollercoaster of emotions from the seventh floor. Her stomach was a crowd of butterflies. She tried to think clearly, but her thoughts wandered to and fro in the maze of her mind.

The brown purse was sitting right by her left foot. The yellow-lined corner of the paper stared back at her while she took deep breaths. She had seen it almost half a dozen times, but she figured one more viewing would help ease her anxiety. The remote footsteps of staff members lingered in the distance.

After covering her eyes and listening to the sounds of her own breath, she finally found the nerve to reach down and pull out the letter. It was a poem written by the patient just over one week earlier. There was just enough light from the half-open doorway for her to read it. She took one more deep breath before looking down at the incredibly neat handwriting. There was not a stirring sound in the room now, and the distant noise seemed to dissipate as she leaned in closer to read the black writing.

*<u>Life of a Teardrop</u>*
*Take me to a place that is forever dawn*
*For it is then I know I have conquered the night.*
*Take me through stars where all else is gone*
*For it is then I know I have ended the fight.*
*Don't look back, don't look back through the fogs of gray,*
*Down through the desolate halls of my memories.*
*There were forsaken lands under a haunted day,*
*There were ghosts and maidens, there were friends and enemies.*
*On a quest through the years, through shadows of grief*
*It was a quest full of wonder, full of failings and grace.*
*There were self-proclaimed sages who promised relief*
*When all I needed was a storm to wash tears from my face.*
*At last I am weightless, falling out of my mind*
*Piece by piece, let me fall through infinity*
*Let me go, let me go back to a time*
*Where fear and love sing a beautiful symphony.*
*Take me to a time with no kings or pawns*
*Where I can find escape, where I can find release*
*Take me to a place that is forever dawn*
*Where the life of a teardrop may finally find peace.*

DOWN THE SIDE of her cheek, she felt the wet trail of a pioneering teardrop. The lump in her throat heightened the emotional weight. Her slow breaths moved her to a distant place where sensation became a monolith. Every moment of joy, anger, and euphoria were all bundled onto one altar where she could worship. The woeful letters helped her feel human again. They created a sense of incredible empathy for her and others.

The existence of her mother's handwriting brought forth an overwhelming longing to read what had been in *her* mind that last few hours. It was an idea that haunted Madelyn's existence; these letters from patients were mere drops from an ocean to quench her thirst. And like saltwater, instead of quenching her craving, they created a bigger need.

Slowly but surely she felt herself rise to the ocean surface. One hand felt the letter being placed back into the purse while she grabbed another set of notes with the other. She felt her white shoes move her to the entrance of the bright hallway.

Her eyes saw the empty rooms all around the corridor. Everyone was preparing to bid goodbye to the final patient of the night. The cool air radiated through every part of her body and mind. She smelled the coffee as she passed the break room and entered the elevator.

The door slid shut and the elevator began to hum its soothing song. Every number was a movement toward an incredible mission. Every breath was a footstep. The number two stayed bright for a few seconds until a blank number occurred. The number four stared back at her. Then finally the number five revealed itself to Madelyn, and off she went to the fire escape to find her accomplice. The digital clock in the hallway read 3:10 a.m.

OUTSIDE ON THE FIRE ESCAPE, Madelyn found herself staring up at the pale face of the half-crescent moon. A few gray clouds crawled across the sky. Her dark hair gently danced with the cool breeze. In the distant cosmos, the stars seemed to shine ever brighter as the night marched on.

The wisdom and the memory of the fiery stars knew no boundaries. They had been there watching when the young earth sprouted forth human life and they would be there watching when all existence returned to dirt. They were timeless. They were the infinite all-seeing witnesses to many things.

Deep within the fantastic cosmos, past the Milky Way, and out beyond the dark galaxies, there was a memory of when Madelyn was much younger, like a rare pearl from a heavenly oyster.

She was eleven years old and found herself spending a peaceful evening with her mother. *Oh to see those glory days once more*, she thought.

Her mother's hair was dark as charcoal and it whisked pleasantly with the gentle wind. They were walking softly on a slightly inclined concrete path. The backdrop was a cloudless night and an incredible stillness to the world. Crickets introduced the close of evening while the sounds of their footsteps pierced the cool atmosphere.

Madelyn followed her mother, as she always did when they visited the place of their monthly ritual. Except this night was to be extraordinary due to a rare occurrence, one that would only happen every thirty-three years. Their excitement was palpable. She looked up to catch a glimpse of her mother stealing a glance back at her daughter.

*That smile*, she thought. *That smile could calm a storm.*

That was her mother: dark skinned; deep brown enchanting eyes that spoke of wisdom.

And if she could freeze that moment, paint a perfect picture encapsulating the face of the gentle beauty before her, then frame it in the halls of the world's most precious treasures, she knew that people would travel from far and wide to view the portrait that everyone called "happiness."

Her mother led the way on the walking path to their destination. They performed an exodus from the city interior towards a hill on the outskirts of Petersburg.

Beyond the silhouette of the hilltop was a collage of yellow stars and distant cosmos waiting for them. Her mother's movements were graceful and full of life. She was an angel indeed.

In this place, nothing seemed to matter except the feeling of blooming curiosity. Her mother believed in the mystery of the cosmos. This was made patent by her studies at the University of Petersburg. An affinity for academic life was heralded in the Hopewell family, and no doubt would be carried on by her daughter.

On this specific night, they were there to witness a comet dancing along its holy brigade across the sky.

And just like that, the angel turned and spoke a soft whisper into Madelyn's ear.

"The stars know a thing or two about all of us." She gently took the girl by the hand. "All we have to do is listen. Come along."

Her voice was velvet, soft and fair, like a morning birdsong after a restless night. Her presence was a beacon in the night, always watching over her daughter.

"Is no one else interested in seeing this?" inquired a newly adolescent Madelyn.

"There hasn't been anyone else for a very long time. I guess it's a treasure for you and me only, my dear."

"Tell me again about the space rock."

"The comet, yes. It travels around the sun every thirty-three years, leaving a meteor shower in its wake. It's like a spaceship blasting its way through the atmosphere with a fiery trail."

"Where did it come from, though?"

The wandering gaze of her mother looked to the heavens as she sighed deeply. After a few still moments, her sweet voice resumed.

"Sit down. I have a story to tell you." She wrapped her arm around Madelyn's shoulder, protecting her from the night, and like that, she developed a sense of warmth between them. The fluffy grass glowed dark blue under the bright moonlight. For one moment, the entire universe made sense. The crickets, the distant bustle of the city, and the wild animals seemed to stop and listen to the voice of her mother.

They sat huddled together on the hilltop with their back to the desolate city. To their side a firm and giant oak tree spread its limbs out, almost as if to worship the stars and the cosmic lights. The gentle breeze was punctured by a soft and enchanting voice.

"A very long time ago," her mother said, "before you and me, before the people in the city, and before civilization, there were gods and goddesses in the heavens above. For eons they looked down upon mortal beings as inferior beasts that had no place among the stars. They regarded the Creator of these beasts as foolish, and the beasts as meant for no great destiny but for hell and anguish."

Madelyn rested her head on her mother's shoulder. The tenderness of her touch erased all anxieties from the world around them.

"The Creator was saddened by all of this. He knew that in the midst of all their flaws was a faint glimmer of hope and glory. But it was too much to be ridiculed by the other gods and goddess, so he took leave. And after he left, the other heavenly beings took notice of his absence.

"At once, the gods and goddesses unleashed their wrath on the tiny planet. They sent down a great meteorite to push the animals to extinction. Fire and brimstone engulfed the earth, leaving few survivors. After the dust settled, a few mortals managed to endure and build again. This only served to enrage the gods, so they sent down plagues and illnesses to punish those who remained. Not only did they scatter them over the earth, they also charmed the humans into greedy and jealous ways to turn them against each other. For millennia, the heavenly beings endeavored to push mortals to the brink of extinction."

Madelyn's mother enjoyed speaking in parables and works of fiction, and here, the silence amplified the master storyteller's intensity.

"But something happened that the gods and goddesses did not expect," she continued. "The survivors of heaven's wrath found within themselves a hidden treasure. They searched deep within their souls and found a new kind of hope in the darkest of places. They found a new reason to live."

Her hand squeezed Madelyn's shoulder. A woeful sigh seemed to push itself from her chest.

"And these people found love. Not only did they fall in love with each other, but they found the greatest weapon of all, which is to fall in love with one's own existence."

"So they fought back. They built communities, they built bridges towards each other, they built roads towards the future, and they built technologies that would take them to new heights. But this disturbed the gods, and angered them. And as one they decided to send forth a world-ending comet, one that the entire universe had never seen."

"The gods ripped off a large piece of rock and sent it hurtling towards the earth. The young mortal beings saw the sky turn crimson, then black. The immense meteor headed right for them and eclipsed their night sky. Men fled, women and children cried out for help, and the animals of the world ran in terror."

"The Creator, who had been gone for centuries, heard the call of his children. So he fled his place of rest and came thundering back to the earth. He saw the giant fiery rock aimed right at it. So he sped up, faster than the speed of light. And he pierced and struck the meteor out of the night sky."

"Down below, the mortal beings looked up to see a fantastic meteor shower before them. It was a heavenly rainfall on their desolate planet. And the creator took what was left of the meteor and flung it into orbit around the sun." Her voice gained in cadence and thunder, adding a more cinematic feel to her story."

"The Creator then decreed that the comet would be the protector of the earth and a symbol of a time when men and women angered the gods by proving that they were worthy of hope and love, but most of all"—her mother paused—"in the midst of a world that never seemed to be meant for them, they found that they were worthy of self-love."

Her mother wrapped her arms around the child. They were kindred hearts, two as one, overlooking a grim city from the pale blue grass beside the loving arms of an oak tree. Above the oak tree stood the black sky of night, speckled with infinite stars and cosmos that witnessed the embrace of a mother and her child.

And just like the Creator himself had come to finish the story, a fantastic view of golden heavens formed above the horizon.

The eyes of both mother and child lit up with awe and wonder at what the twilight was about to reveal. And then they both saw the incoming attraction that had brought them there.

Beyond the black horizon a dazzling comet pushed its

way through the soft air. If the night sky was an ocean, the comet was a golden pebble skimming along the surface, leaving golden ripples in its wake.

Madelyn felt the deep breaths of her mother. The world had never seemed so peaceful. She thought about what the comet meant, and what humans could be capable of.

Beyond the comet stood an audience of constellations. Beyond the constellations were galaxies and planets far beyond the reach of imagination.

The dream sequence dissolved in the memory of Madelyn Hopewell as she was brought back to earth staring into the same night sky that she and her mother had on that night in 2031.

Waiting on the fire escape for her accomplice, she held the memory like a rare pearl. And she wished to again be under the oak tree, staring into the chaotic eternal, wondering about self-love and what it could do for them.

**13**

———

Dr. Cotham and her associates were busy chatting about expansionary plans. The top-floor employees had congregated together in the conference room, surrounding the large wooden circular table. The government officials took joy in becoming part of the ceremony, despite being incredibly exhausted from the night's events. A few yawns were passed around the room as coffee mugs were lifted and dropped to the table with measured movements.

The director stood in front of the group and swiped at the holographic display. All present looked in awe at the future institutions designed by the architects and Dr. Cotham. The hologram shone its pale blue light onto her face, revealing a triumphant smile.

"And before we adjourn to our departments for the final Mirage program of the night"—she swiped one last time and stood tall—"I just want to say how proud I am of how far we've come. When talented people come together to build monuments that help us understand ourselves better, there is nothing that can stop us. The work done here at the first institution is only the beginning."

Most present nodded in agreement at Dr. Cotham's victory speech. All present felt the energy in her voice. There was music in her tone.

"And," she continued, "I want to thank each and every one of you for getting us here. And I especially want to thank the government for believing in us also. My colleagues, please stand!"

A warm applause rebounded through the whole room as the three men rose. Handshakes were dispersed to the staff members around them. Dr. Cotham smiled as her hands clapped together for everything that they had built. An unholy symphony was playing out on the top floor.

THE OUTSIDE AIR seemed to grow thick with despair, and Madelyn tasted it deeply while she awaited for Errol's call. A low knock startled her. She turned to see the steel gray door open slowly. It creaked ever so quietly. A hand appeared around the edge and then his face. His solid frame followed with a warm smile.

"Hello, Madelyn."

"Hello." She stepped forward and abruptly hugged Errol. This interrupted his calm entrance; he stood there with his hands up, then finally wrapped them around her.

After a few moments, they separated. She looked down while searching for words to fit the occasion.

"I want to thank you for this, Errol," she finally said. "There's not a lot of trust in this world anymore. It's good to see it still exists."

"Especially in a place like this one. A lot of virtues can be lost," he said warmly.

"How has your night been so far?"

"Uneventful." He let out slight laugh that made Madelyn

smile along with him. "A person shouldn't get used to what happens on that third floor. But after a few of them, the human spirit adapts. It's like elastic."

"Did you expect it to be any different when you started working here?"

"You know, I don't know what I expected, really. Maybe after this internship I'll move on—though there's not a lot left for scientists out there anymore." He looked out at the trees. "I was thinking maybe the military."

"Same industry, I suppose."

"Exactly." He pulled out a small device from his pocket. "Listen, we should probably get going before the patient moves into the Mirage room. Here's that earpiece."

She held it with two fingers, and then pushed it into her earlobe. She could hear a small murmur and chatting, but from where?

"Sorry, one second," said Errol. He waved his hand in front of his own earpiece and spoke into it. "Jose, do you copy?"

"I thought you said we were using code names?" snapped Jose in a threatening whisper that came through clearly to Madelyn in her own earpiece.

"Never mind—there's nobody else on this line. Are we clear so far?"

"Yeah, we're good. The overlords on the seventh floor are just settling down for the final show, and I've been feeding them a false TV feed for the past half-hour."

"Brilliant, so we can get off this line, then."

"Ten four, over and out, comrade." Jose's voice faded out. Errol smiled at Madelyn.

The wind swayed through the trees as it traveled between them. Her heart seemed to skip a few beats whenever she was around him. There was a certain kind of safety that he gave her whenever he was around.

"So..." He breathed deeply. *This is it*, he thought. "Once you get down to that third floor and in through the fire escape, you will see a small hatch door. On the other side will be your patient." His gracious smirk arrested her attention. "When it's close to three-thirty, I'll let you know."

"Okay. You and Jose seem to know everything about this place."

"As a scientist I'm curious by nature. Believe me, a *lot* of us have information about the Complex that we shouldn't have."

"A lot of virtues are lost in this place. I guess it's human nature." A gentle smile appeared on her face. "But I suppose the time has come. I should get going."

She turned around and stopped. The moon shone ever brighter. She turned around again and kissed him on the lips. This startled him even more than the previous hug. For one brief moment, the entire world seemed to make sense while they shared an intimate embrace.

A crash echoed through the cold night. The fire escape door slammed against the wall. Bright lights pierced the black abyss, blinding him. A figure towered in the doorway.

"And where do you think you two are going?" came the sinister voice of Ms. Cross.

Errol and Madelyn simultaneously pushed away from each other. Errol felt his face stuck in shock and horror, like an animal frozen at the sight of headlights. Their clandestine plans were uncovered, laid bare for Ms. Cross to see. Errol's heart sank.

"You didn't think that in a place like this anything would be kept secret..." Her footsteps rang hollow through the night, heavy feet on metal, the march of a general in wartime, one presiding over a court martial.

Her beady black eyes glanced over at Errol. He would be her first victim.

"Mr. Winters. I saw you in the break room thinking about this meeting on the fire escape. Has it happened just as you imagined it would?"

"Not exactly," he replied nervously.

"Wait inside," she ordered him. "I will deal with you later."

The tension in the air eclipsed all other emotions. Errol stood frozen in place. Next to him, Madelyn had anchored herself onto the railing and was breathing in short gusts.

"Look, I—"

"Now!" Ms. Cross took a step toward him. "I can call Security to help you move, if that's what you wish."

He relaxed his shoulders in defeat and glanced toward Madelyn. *I'm sorry*, he thought. The night air escaped into the building, door moving slowly inward, his body moving mechanically through it while his mind searched for answers. This was a horrible nightmare. He was falling infinitely. When the door shut behind him, he leaned up against the wall and sighed deeply. The silence deafened his thoughts. He truly felt alone.

And now Madelyn felt truly alone.

"So tell me about your little crusade, Ms. Hopewell, star employee scheduled to take over as assistant director of her department. I heard about that before it happened." The record keeper's shrill voice punctured the peaceful night. More footsteps on metal raised the pulse of the person she was interrogating.

"It was nothing," Madelyn said. "We were just out here talking about the promotion." She looked down. An awkward alibi was no match for what the evil woman had as evidence against them. She wondered if Errol was listening through his earpiece or if he had given up.

"Ha! For someone who specializes in understanding the human condition, you really are terrible at making up lies."

A sudden footstep on the fire escape shortened the distance between them. "Now tell me, what were you planning to do?"

"It was just going to be a conversation with the patient, nothing more," Madelyn said quickly. A sudden surge of bravery coursed through her veins. "You would be doing the exact same thing if you were in my position. Spending all this time watching and reading about the person only increases curiosity."

"It's not about what *I* would do. In fact," said Ms. Cross, "I'm in perfect alignment with my job duties, which is uncovering people's destructive habits."

"And mine is to understand the patients much better."

"So you have done this by giving that man in there their confidential letters for the past few months? Yes, I have been watching that too." Ms. Cross waited to let that sink in. "I even saw the neat little handoff under the table in the break room."

Anger rose in Madelyn. "But why wait until the last moment? If you knew before, then that puts *you* in breach of duties."

"I wanted to build this case slowly, just so Dr. Cotham could see how far you willing to go to destroy the integrity of this place."

"You're evil, just like the rest of them on the top floor." Madelyn couldn't keep the frustration from making her voice quiver.

"Finally, a little anger from the talented Miss Hopewell! Everybody's favorite intern—her credentials so sparkling that she is held in high regard by the evil ones on the top floor. You know I have been here since day one and haven't been considered for one promotion? I have been locked on the second floor, diligently filing away letter after letter, hoping to be lifted to the top."

"Is *that* what this is about?" asked Madelyn, finding new strength.

"Not entirely. I have built a strong case against you and your lovestruck accomplice in there. But more importantly"—her eyes narrowed—"throughout these years, brooding over my purpose as record keeper, stoking the fires of despair while reading the thousands and thousands of death wishes in those letters, realizing that petty guilt isn't enough to push back against the immense evil that has eclipsed this world... More importantly, I have built a case against this malicious institution."

The bitter wind gently retreated so the stars and the blissful night could listen along with her confession.

Madelyn's breath came short. "What?"

"You seem to be the most intelligent person in the Complex, but your reclusive habits prevent you from getting to know people fully. We all have fallen so far we don't even recognize each other, nor even try to. This entire world has gone mad, I know. But our response is to exploit people when they are at their most vulnerable—have them write letters, talk to a merciless machine, and then push them off the edge. I don't know if that is justice, but I know that there has got to be a better way. I stand here accused of being one of the most evil beings you have ever met, but it's not *me* who is manufacturing a death machine and calling it mercy!" Her voice towered above the treetops and echoed throughout the heavens. This was followed by a great and hideous silence.

Ms. Cross looked away. She stole a glance at the night sky and let a deep sigh. "I don't mean to hurt anybody, but tell me, Madelyn." Her glassy, weary eyes caught Madelyn's stare. "What is her name?" she asked.

"Who?"

"Please, I am tired of these one-word answers."

Ms. Cross let out another deep sigh. "Your mother—what is her name?"

"Her name is Maria," Madelyn found herself saying. "Maria Hopewell. Why is this important right now?" she asked desperately. No one in those walls had ever dared bring up her past! It belonged only to those who needed to know it.

Ms. Cross nodded her head with something that resembled a smile on her lips. Then, awkwardly, hesitantly, she pulled something from out of her pocket. Finally, with great effort, she removed a letter from a brown envelope. Her hand was quivering.

"Here." For the first time, she smiled at Madelyn. "I think this belongs to you."

In Madelyn's hand, she now held the whole universe. A new and great power had been bestowed upon her entire existence, a power of knowing and finally understanding. For years, she had been lost in an existential desert—lost, wandering, and thirsting for answers. Now an unlikely ally had given all that power to her. The letter felt like fifty pounds of lead. Her hand was quivering.

Slowly and painfully, she unfolded the aged letter. On the top of the page, above cursive handwritten sentences, was a date: September 3, 2034. One day after this, the authorities would find her mother's body. Two days after that, they would seize all of her mother's belongings in a vain attempt to erase the memory of all of the anguish. For three days, Madelyn would sit outside her mother's room, waiting to hear her breath, crying and weeping for all that was lost and taken from her.

Finally, on the fourth day, she would realize that pain and suffering are virtues just like justice and mercy. So she would live with it. She would bear the burden of never knowing and hold onto it, until that very moment out on the fire escape. Her body was water. She was weightless. She folded the paper without reading it and regarded the new ally who stood across from her.

The gentle breeze picked up again. The treetops whispered and the moonlight glistened off the metal frame.

"Thank you." A tear traveled down her left cheek. "So you knew all along?"

"Do you think you're the only one with ghosts? I lost someone when I was young, too." Ms. Cross seemed to stare into the abyss, like a veteran recalling war stories. "But look, that doesn't mean we have to be consenting elements in this evil game they are playing. I've tried to find redemption, but if I can give peace to someone who needs it, then that is sufficient." She calmly stepped closer to Madelyn and placed her hand on her shoulder.

From a person she had felt so coldly toward, a sudden warmth embraced Madelyn. Ms. Cross smiled and placed her hand on top of the letter. At once, she was transformed into a friendly sage.

"Read it when you're ready," she said softly. "There are few things left that are sacred in this world. And your mother's thoughts are the most of them."

Before Madelyn knew it, Ms. Cross was halfway toward the fire escape door. Their short spell of friendship was broken as reality came crashing down.

"It seems," Ms. Cross said, "that I've delayed you significantly, but there is still time to talk to *him*." She opened the door. "You must get going."

Errol stood up quickly from where he had slumped to the ground as mysteries were unraveled, coming up with his own exit strategy. *What does she have to talk to* me *about?* he wondered. But this thought dissolved the moment he saw the smile on Ms. Cross's face.

"And *you*," she said to him. "Make sure she gets out in

time." Her slender body moved to the side to allow Madelyn to enter from the cold night. The moon and stars bade them goodnight for the moment.

Ms. Cross's small body seemed to float along the tiled floor, her light steps carrying it toward the corridor. Madelyn watched in astonishment as the woman she realized was not so old after all transformed into a wise friend, an unlikely ally in a galaxy of despair, a teaspoon of honey in a world full of tar. This new bond gave her hope. She looked over at Errol, who was holding the door open; there was hope in his eyes, too. She was about to say one last word of encouragement to him before she left when the soft voice of Ms. Cross came back again.

"And Madelyn..." She turned around slightly. "His name is Anthony."

"The patient?"

"Yes. His name is Anthony." The black uniform carrying her body disappeared around the corner.

Outside, the chaotic moon and stars prepared for the night's final proceedings. They watched and waited as the door to that malicious institution closed. Its inhabitants sat down at desks, exhaustedly glancing at reports or staring at screens. None of them had any idea of the clandestine and covert operations that were unfolding on the third floor, the one without windows.

It was a building with no redeeming qualities, save for the one soul destined to dive deep into the mysteries of the human condition. Madelyn said a thank-you, walked down the fire escape to the third floor, opened the steel door, stole a glance toward the night sky, breathed deeply, and dissolved into the dark chamber.

**14**

———————

In the holding chamber, Anthony stared at the white light hovering above his head. This artificial sun was his only warmth. His only comfort was staring at the light. In the metal chair, his gray T-shirt moved gently along with his deep breathing. The blue jeans led to bare feet on the concrete floor. His gaze wandered to the wall in front of him where the door would eventually open. He closed his eyes and listened to the sound of his breathing. In his mind, he heard the distant sounds of footsteps. They slowly became less frequent as he tried to shake what he was hearing. Then suddenly the sound of the hatch door caught his full attention. It slowly creaked open and in walked a young woman wearing a navy blue uniform, her head lowered.

At this point, he didn't know whether to trust in his own vision, or to trust in anything, for that matter. So he just let it happen.

"Hello." His soft voice filled the room.

After a few tense moments, Madelyn looked up and saw a young man staring back at her. The white light revealed dark hair neatly cut short, deep-set eyes with a hint of blue, and a square jaw that held above it a gentle smile. His hands held the arms of the chair as he turned ever so slightly.

"Hello." She spoke equally as softly. "My name is Madelyn. I am one of the psychologists who works here." She pointed to her nametag, with the familiar insignia.

The hatch door let out a slight click as it was closed. Their voices echoed slightly and pierced the empty silence.

"My name is Anthony", he reported to the incoming stranger. "I suppose you already know who I am." As a patient constantly underneath the analytical spotlight of machines and intelligence, he was somewhat bewildered to see sentient life make one final appearance.

"Nice to meet you, Anthony. I apologize if I have startled you." Their eyes locked. Madelyn saw a world that was waiting to be unlocked, but a world that was content with everything around it. Anthony saw a world full of questions, for them both.

THE INTERNS behind Errol were preparing for the final program. He sat down and got comfortable with his surroundings. His papers were scattered about on his desk, so he began to look for an empty one. Madelyn's voice was his background music for the next few moments. She sang a sweet melody through the earpiece. He could also hear the voice of a young man; he seemed enchanted by Madelyn.

"IT'S OKAY," Anthony said. "These days, nothing seems to bother me anymore." He looked to the floor.

"Anthony, I just have a few questions I would like to go through with you. Is that okay?"

She leaned down and took his hand. The euphoric touch was something that he had not felt in a very long time. The caring voice of FATE seemed to diminish against the feeling of human connection. Although the celestial voice of an advanced intelligence calmed the storms beneath him, it was this moment that provided him a life raft. It awakened something within him, and he looked back up at her. She had the kind of eyes that said, *Tell me a story.* Her voice was soft, symphonic, and human.

"They told me no more interviews. But if this can help the others in any way, then yes. I am all ears, Madelyn." He smiled.

"Okay. And if you feel uncomfortable at all, please let me know."

Madelyn's heart rate began its slow ascent. She pulled out a paper and pen from one of her pockets. The crisp vintage paper of her mother's letter sat untouched in the other pocket.

"Anthony, do you know where you are right now?"

He sighed deeply and sank back into the chair. "In a facility somewhere in Petersburg. I don't really remember much about getting here, but I heard whispers about this place before I was submitted."

"And do you know how long you have been here?"

"It's difficult because all the days bleed into one another. But I would have to recall through the letters I have wrote. The first one was dated..." His eyes wandered to the ceiling. "Most likely seven months ago? Yeah, I've been here seven months now."

"Okay. And how would you describe this place?"

After one long breath his eyes darted side to side, as if they were searching for something, and then the corner of his lips gently moved upward.

"Well," he began, "it is new territory for the collective

mind, I suppose. I have been taken care of in this place. It seems nobody dislikes me, and the walls don't yell back. I have been given the chance to explore parts of my mind that I wouldn't have on the outside." His gaze wandered toward Madelyn. "It's a place where people don't wait for their turn to speak. FATE has been one of the most important allies for me. The institution listens. They all listen. *You* listen. That's part of it. But I suppose the significance lies in the belief that sometimes escape is necessary. It's a place not without ideology, but I suppose it's a place that's not afraid to ask the right questions."

"So perhaps listening is a key part in forming the proper questions. Has FATE done more than just listen to you?" Madelyn inquired. She was looking for a thoughtful review from someone who had spent hours upon hours with the advanced AI.

"Oh yes!" he exclaimed. "It seems to be a machine without ego, without pride or arrogance. It ceases to be anything else but a companion to talk to, and it responds with the highest degree of knowledge of psychology. I guess it offers new way to look at things, to reframe cognitive outlooks that may be harmful to someone like myself."

"And how do you feel right now, after many encounters with FATE, Anthony?" she asked.

After a short pause, he looked up.

"Content. It's something I've not felt in a very long time. My entire life, I felt like my mind was trapped in a dungeon, like my mind was haunted. Every task and every breath was empty. Every day is a small step for humanity, but for me it was a giant one. Every moment was a battle to find meaning. But talking to someone like FATE who seems to be a supreme being in its own right has, I suppose, shown me how advanced technology is the only way to salvation from suffering. And now, right now, Madelyn? I feel fulfilled."

❧

Errol leaned back into his chair while absorbing what Anthony had said. His tone emanated a calm found only on distant mountains. *He does seem satisfied*, he thought. He looked to his watch as Madelyn continued.

❧

"And can you tell me how you felt before you entered this place?"

"Yes." A deep sigh escaped him.

The paper in Madelyn's hand began to shake slightly as she wrote down a few notes but Anthony was only enamored by the look in her eyes. It made him feel safe and at peace with what was about to happen to him. He had never felt the touch of solace just from the look in someone's eyes. This alien feeling began to form deep within him while he thought about life before the Complex.

"I had no desire to talk to anybody," he began, "yet I was incredibly lonely. Social gatherings were always a mountain I needed to climb. All the 'Hello, how are you' seemed empty and hollow. The only time I was happy was heading for the exit signs. So I remained secluded. It began with one day off from my job, then two, and finally those days began to fade into each other. No phone calls. I didn't feel alive anymore. I just felt like a tourist within my own heart, body, and mind."

After a few silent moments, Madelyn finished jotting down a few notes then asked, "This feeling of not being alive anymore—when did that start, Anthony?"

"I would say that the idea began to consume me after my twentieth birthday. I am twenty-four right now, so it was about a sixth of my life. It began with the little things—a painting, perhaps. Where someone would see beauty in the lines or elegance in the colors, my mind would see a wasteland. It would refuse to grasp the feeling in it. From there, it seemed my entire world was black and white, without elegance and artistry. I also grew up in a musical household. Played the violin for the Petersburg Symphony at one time. Where someone would hear life in the notes or joy and pleasure in the melody, my mind would hear nothing but torturous noise. It became a burden to hear some of my favorite songs. That's when it began to take hold of me. All the important stuff seemed to fade away into oblivion."

Madelyn's pulse ascended. The sweat on her palms returned. She recalled the history of this young man before her. He had been far removed from her in the letters and interviews she studied; being up close and personal with him was surreal. No training could have prepared her for this type of inquisition. But she felt an incredible urge to continue.

"Did you ever explore where these feelings manifested themselves?" she asked.

"I thought about that long and hard. It's like asking what was there before light appeared in the universe. It's a strange phenomenon when it does happen. I can't think straight about anything, really. Perhaps it's a chemical imbalance that can be remedied only by the right medication, but I think it goes deeper than that."

Madelyn was conscious of the scratch of her pen on the paper in her hand and of the white light staring down on both of them. When she was done, she looked back up. Anthony had turned his gaze toward the door in front of him.

"When you say 'deeper,' what do you mean?" she asked.

"I mean subconsciously there could be something that triggers it. Something that happens in the outer world could also lead to a dark premonition in one's soul. Especially today, when governments have declared what's happening as an epidemic. This world is far removed from what it once was. But perhaps we are the architects of this all—this social decay that has been slowly rotting us for centuries. We have introduced the parasite that we're trying to escape from. We cannot contain the rot that lives within. So most of us escape into digital realms, never knowing the gold that lies beneath. We have built panic rooms to live in. And those of us who fall victim to this callous social order, those of us who wish death upon themselves, *we* are the ones who need to be studied?"

ERROL THOUGHT BACK to his own time in the darkness, and thought about how the feeling of social decay paralleled his own ideas of why the world was the way it was. He regarded Anthony as a philosopher who seemed to create a theory for all the world's different problems, just as he did. But he also thought that living through depressive episodes provides a person with something most people never have: perspective. Errol held onto every word he was hearing, while his colleagues seemed glued to the work in front of them.

ANTHONY MOVED CLOSER to the edge of his seat, clenching onto the arms of the chair. The look in his eyes became intense fire as he stared at the door.

"No. Today, we live in a world where people are a means to an end. And it has me thinking me, Madelyn." His flaming eyes turned to her. "Perhaps *we* are not the ones who are mentally ill."

She stepped back, holding her mouth. The calm inner composure she had summoned earlier had vanished, but she could not step back again: she needed the light. After a few short scribbles, the interview continued.

"And this place you are in right now has been one of the trigger points?" she asked as calmly as possible.

"Not necessarily. I *have* dwelled upon a few things while doing these talk therapy sessions with FATE. One thing we talked about is happiness, and what kind of virtues we need to live a life fulfilled. I have learned that happiness is just controlling fear. For so much of my life I have tried to create order. Create order here! Create order there! It has consumed me. But what if it isn't about that? Life isn't about creating order; rather, it's about adapting to the chaos. So much of the world is chaos right now. And I know that the second I walk into that room in front of me and hit the button on the other side to start the program"—he pointed in front of him, his hand slightly shaking—"Once I do that, then I know that I have truly harnessed the power of my fear. I have taken it, battled with it, and learned so much about the world and myself. I have found something within the suffering. Somehow, Madelyn, I have found happiness and can finally rest in peace."

ERROL LOOKED at his watch and realized they were getting short on time. He leaned in closer to his desk with his head down. "Madelyn, we have five minutes left. Please start wrapping it up now."

THE PSYCHOLOGIST SCRIBBLED some notes and began walking

around the room. The white gleaming light pushed her in and out of Anthony's view. He sat back into his chair and again a deep sigh escaped him.

"When you talk about harnessing the power of your fear," she said, "what do you mean by that?"

"It feels like it's been a lifetime of being paralyzed by fear. Sometimes it kept me in bed for days—getting out of that chamber seemed like a triumph. I never thought about death while in the darkest depths of my mind, but it does come from there. Fear and death are empty companions at first. Then they start talking."

Madelyn looked over at him. His lower lip had begun to quiver; his arms were shaking.

"Anthony, are you okay?"

"Yes. I'm fine. We can continue. It's okay." After the piercing silence, and after he had pinched the bridge of his nose, breathing heavily, the interview carried on. Everyone in the building breathed together in anticipation of Anthony's entering the Mirage program. The building stood silent as the interview raged on.

"Here's the thing," the patient declared. "From the outside, people think it's cowardice and weakness. But if what I am doing is weakness, then I don't want to be strong. Strength isn't about disregarding fear and dismissing it out of hand—it's not about overcoming it. It's about acknowledging its immense presence over all of us and learning how to use it. Fear becomes you. And the reason why I'm here today, in this facility, is not because I want to die. I don't want to die. All I know is that I do not want to be here anymore."

"Well, where would you *like* to be, Anthony?"

More hideous silence filled the small chamber.

"Released from the prison of my mind."

Madelyn's eyes met Anthony's piercing gaze. His body

was strong and healthy, like he was ready to be deployed for a war. There was no cowardice or weakness to him. He had the demeanor of a king out for conquest, his resolved strengthened by the bold questions being asked to him in the last moments of his life.

"Thank you, Anthony," she said. "Just a few more questions, if I may. It seems you have a firm grasp on what we do here at the Complex. As one of the lead psychologists, what if I told you that we are working on an alternative therapy?"

~

ERROL'S EYEBROWS rose at this last question. He cautiously whispered into the earpiece, "Madelyn, what are you doing?"

~

THE PAPER in her hand began to shake.

Anthony stared straight ahead and attempted to collect his thoughts.

"I am content," he said, "with this place and the program. Any other kind of release would feel artificial." His gaze slowly wandered to the floor.

She continued to walk around the chair. The silence hung between them as she wrote down a few further notes.

"FATE loves to talk about virtues, I'm told. Virtue may be part of it, but it's not the entire thing. Anthony, in this session with myself as another person, listening to you and breathing in the same air, how does it make you feel?"

The bewilderment gave way to premonition, as if he had thought of a grand idea to share with the world. His eyes looked in wonder at the windows of Madelyn's soul. The alien feeling of solace seemed to push itself through his body. "I suppose it does have more meaning than talking to a machine. It truly does feel better."

"Then just a little belief is all you need." Her approach to delegitimizing the artificial intelligence's seemed rooted in her own disdain for the counseling session she had had to endure. But she felt an urge to not probe this further with Anthony, so she pulled out a familiar piece of paper and set it in front of him.

"In your poem," she then said, "this place you look for, where the stars are gone and it's forever dawn—can you tell me about it?"

This gave him pause as his mouth began to move. His eyes became glassy as he looked up at Madelyn.

"Poetry gives me wings, but it's the world that takes away the skies. It provides me an avenue by which to escape, a world that I can dream up and find brief moments of solace in an island among an ocean of despair. I read in a book once that the prisoners in World War II concentration camps would hold cabarets full of song and poetry. Can you imagine that? In a life full of pain and suffering they found art in a desolate place, always holding onto what was beautiful in their own hearts. I cannot imagine the horrors they endured, but I can only assume they understood what the human spirit needed in that moment. It is that same process that I cling to: writing poetry. So when I say that I am searching for something, it's no place in particular, just a mirage of my own, I suppose. It's also not a desire for anybody. It wasn't a person, Madelyn. I desired a utopia of my own design—a place of release, where a teardrop can finally find peace."

As Madelyn walked behind him she leaned in behind his shoulder. She softly whispered, "Where fear and love sing a beautiful symphony."

Tears began to fall down his cheek.

"It really is beautiful verse, Anthony," she said. Suddenly she felt the spell of her own interrogation breaking down. A large, luminous proverbial wall had been struck down by her inquisitiveness. Their spirits became one as Madelyn tried to force back images of her own mother. She imagined talking to her as if she were right there in the room with them. Then she anchored herself with the breathing; it was always the breathing.

Anthony sat further up on his chair and leaned toward her. A warm concern washed over his eyes as he grabbed her by the hand. Tears still fell.

"Madelyn, are you okay?"

"Yes, I'm fine. It's just been a long night." Flashes of the train struck through her mind. She fought back against the urge to retreat and carried on with new vigor.

"You talk about becoming fear, but not about becoming love," she said gently. "Becoming one is becoming the other. It is possible to exist with both of them, right here in this world. Just like light needs darkness to exist, so do fear and love need each other. Anthony, there is something in you that the world is much darker without. No patient who passes through these doors leaves, and because of that the world becomes less beautiful. FATE will never understand this because it is a machine. An intelligent machine, yes, but intelligence without compassion is tyranny. You talk about writing poetry as a way to amuse the demons within you and as a way to draw up a utopia for your soul—then do that. I am here to tell you that you can fight, that there is a lot left in this reality for you. This world is not done with you yet."

Their spirits seemed to eclipse the entire universe around them. They were an immovable force within that small chamber. The white lamp overhead swayed slightly back and forth. Madelyn felt sweat forming on her forehead. She felt strength unbound between them.

And Anthony felt something he had not experienced in a lifetime. He felt his arms and legs fall free of the spiritual shackles he was captive in. A sudden urge to live overwhelmed him. He stared into the paradise in her eyes. They were kind of eyes that could calm a storm. They were eyes that had known what losing feels like. They were eyes that had suffered. He felt as if he were looking into a mirror.

"My brain says there's nothing for me out there anymore, but that could be another mirage overtaking my truest desires. I cannot trust it. My heart speaks of something else, and that I can trust." Tears spoke of pain, yet they washed away a deeper suffering from within him.

She leaned in closer to him and grabbed him by both shoulders. "What if I told you there was another way out of here? That life can be given back to you tonight?"

~

Errol calmly walked out of the lab, his heart beating violently. It was not until he was in the hallway that he frantically searched for words to counsel Madelyn with. "Okay, Madelyn. Time is up. I'm coming in there!" He walked briskly down the corridor. The few colleagues in nearby labs took little notice of his sudden departure toward the fire escape.

~

Anthony wiped away a tear then stared at the moisture on his hand. It somehow meant life to him. It somehow meant the entire world was opening itself up to him. He stared ahead at the door. Madelyn stood beside him, waiting, breathing.

He whispered, "Take me to a place that is forever dawn, where the life of a teardrop may finally find peace."

In the dark chamber, he rose from the chair where he had been confined. And with him, a new hope rose.

A new day appeared.

A distant song called out his name in the wilderness.

Out beyond the institution and beyond the forest that surrounded it, there was something for him. He didn't know what, but there was in him an insatiable urge to find it. It consumed it. It became him.

In the bitter darkness, he finally said, "Take me there."

She put her hand on his shoulder.

"Anthony. Follow me."

ERROL RAN down the corridor and toward the fire escape. "Madelyn!" he said into the air. He didn't hear anything on the other side of the earpiece. *She must have turned it off*, he thought.

He pushed himself through the exit and into the night-time darkness. The crisp air enveloped his body. Another door clicked open. Swift footsteps on metal punctured the night air: not far from him, people were running. He hurried his steps down the fire escape toward the third floor, then past it. His heart beat ever more violently. His legs were fire and his breath could barely contain the sudden gusts of oxygen pumping through it. He moved back and forth down the fire escape until his feet met the black soil of the ground.

The moon illuminated the hideous view. He felt a few drops of rain as he took a few moments to catch his breath.

When he turned to find the escapees, shock overwhelmed him.

He was chasing not two people but one. The imprints of a man's bare feet separated the ground between Errol and the runner. In the distance, he saw the man running for his life, and at the same time toward his life. Madelyn was not with him.

Errol ran back to the fire escape. Up past the first floor, he whispered her name. Up past the second floor, he shouted her name. And finally, when he reached the third floor, he screamed her name.

As he ran inside and toward the holding chamber, his heart was jumping out of his chest. He felt the whole world pushing in on him. Then he felt a sudden shortness of breath: the hatch door to the holding chamber was open. His footsteps quickened.

"Madelyn!" Nothing.

"Madelyn!" he said more softly. Still nothing.

He turned the corner and looked in. Fear seized his whole body.

The chair in the middle was empty. The lamp swayed ever so gently above. His eyes darted to each corner and found nothing.

Then, across from him, the door of the Mirage room slid shut. And in the window of the door, to his terror, he saw the face of Madelyn on the other side.

He ran with the strength of a mighty wind across the chamber, ran to his love on the other side.

Madelyn looked out the window. She could see the fear in his eyes as his mouth screamed out her name. His fist pounded on the glass. He tried to look for a knob or lever to pry the door open. She watched as he helplessly threw the chair at the glass, tears flowing from his eyes. She watched him mouth her name. Her gentle, warm eyes regarded him with admiration. But it was too late.

Madelyn stood there on the other side with her hand against the glass. The white fog surrounded her. She smiled warmly, let out a long breath, turned around, and walked away.

In her office above, Dr. Cotham watched in horror as Madelyn pushed the button to start the Mirage program. She yelled at her staff to cut the feed. She ran out into the hallway and screamed out orders to everyone around her. The government officials were escorted out of the building by security officers. Shocked interns began to cry at the piercing alarm. The Complex went into lockdown as medical officers rushed helplessly to the third floor.

Outside, sirens wailed in the distance. Outside, a cold bitterness gripped the atmosphere as the heavens began to rain down on that dark and bitter building.

## 15

———

After shock and despair came appalling silence. All seven floors of the Complex were lit up from inside, except the one without windows. On the third floor, a clock on the wall said 5:30 a.m.

By then, the authorities had cleared out everyone except senior-level staff members, who were handcuffed and undergoing interrogation onsite.

Down the third-floor corridor, through the hatch door of the holding chamber, and through the entrance to the Mirage room was a large padded room with a still body in it.

Madelyn lay there in her navy uniform with her bare feet crossed. One arm lay across her chest. With her other hand, she held her mother's letter, gripping onto a corner. On her face she wore a smile.

It portrayed a life unbroken but gone from the earth too soon. It portrayed the life of a sleeping beauty. She had finally found peace.

OVER THE HORIZON the sun began to show her face. The

orange dawn spoke of a restless night that was no more. The morning air outside that grim building breathed freely as it introduced the day.

And in that part of the world, another empire had fallen.

And in the heavens above, another supernova was no more.

Another star had faded.

# EPILOGUE

S oft steps on the wondrous earth were the morning song of a brand-new day. Green fields of misty grass stretched out towards the horizon. Up the hill, he appeared to float along the colorful landscape. Behind him, the brown treeline bade goodbye to the traveler who had just left the embrace of the forest.

He felt his vision returning. The world seemed to present itself in new shades of orange and blue. And as he found the top of the hill, he took a seat beneath the loving arms of an oak tree.

He felt an absolute sense of peace descend upon him, as if there were angels watching over him. The city stretched out behind him. The cloudless sky presented an extravagant blue and purple mosaic, promising that the night of mourning would soon be over.

And above the horizon, there rose the most beautiful star that ever existed. It was a star that promised to never forsake those who sought refuge in watching it rise every morning.

In that moment, he began to believe in the value of the

morning star. He felt self-worth and self-love beginning to blossom within his soul.

And as he smiled deeply, he took in a breath of the beautiful, magnificent life he found himself living in.

And in the still morning, he thought to himself, *Everything is okay. Everything will be okay.*

# AFTERWORD

This was a tough one to write.

The manuscript went through many variations in an attempt to make the literature as risk-free as possible. I read books, referred to blogs, and watched many videos on how to approach a book that deals with sensitive subject matter.

But this is all just surface level stuff, and I am by no means an expert on the matter.

Having gone through counselling myself, I am convinced that there is hope for anyone out there looking for help.

*Just a little belief is all you need,* according to Madelyn.

(Yes, I just quoted one of my own characters.)

This book is also not an exercise in frontier psychology and therefore, nothing can replace the guidance of mental health experts.

So in that spirit, if you or anyone you know is thinking about suicide, then what follows are helpful resources.

These are the <u>true</u> professionals who are available to assist you.

This is not an exhaustive list and with each edition of the book, new resources will be available (Canadian phone numbers only).

**National Resources for Information about Mental Health and Therapy**

*Canadian Mental Health Association*
   416-646-5557

*Canadian Psychological Association*
   1-888-472-0657

*Mental Health Commission*
   613-683-3755

*Canadian Association for Suicide Prevention*
   204-784-4073

**National Crisis Hotlines**

*Canada Drug Rehab Addiction Services Directory*
   1-866-462-6362

*Centre for Suicide Prevention*
   1-833-456-4566

*Crisis Services Canada*

1-833-456-4566, or text 45645

*First Nations and Inuit Hope for Wellness Help Line*
1-855-242-3310

*Kids Help Phone*
1-800-668-6868

*National Eating Disorder Information Centre*
1-866-633-4220

*Native Youth Crisis Hotline*
1-877-209-1266

**Resources by Province**

**British Columbia**

*Adlerian Psychology Association of B.C.*
604-742-1818

*B.C. Association of Clinical Counsellors*
1-800-909-6303

*Crisis Centre*
1-800-784-2433

*Canadian Mental Health Association - British Columbia Division*
1-800-555-8222

**Alberta**

*Psychologists's Association of Alberta*
1-888-424-0297

*Distress Centre*
   403-266-4357

*Canadian Mental Health Association - Alberta Division*
   780-482-6576

**Sakatchewan**

*Saskatchewan College of Psychologists*
   306-352-1699

*Saskatoon Crisis Intervention Service*
   306-933-6200

*Canadian Mental Health Association - Saskatchewan Division*
   1-800-461-5483

**Manitoba**

*Manitoba Psychological Society*
   204-488-7398

*Manitoba Crisis Line*
   1-888-322-3019

*Canadian Mental Health Association - Manitoba Division*
   204-982-6100

**Ontario**

*Ontario Society of Psychotherapists*
   416-923-4050

*Ontario Mental Health Helpline*

1-866-531-2600

*Canadian Mental Health Association - Ontario Division*
    416-977-5580

**Quebec**

*Action on Mental Illness*
    1-877-303-0264

*Centre de Prevention du Suicide de Quebec*
    1-866-277-3553

**Newfoundland and Labrador**

*Mobile Crisis Response Team*
    1-888-737-4668

*Canadian Mental Health Association - Newfoundland and Labrador Division*
    1-877-753-8550

**New Brunswick**

*Chimo Helpline*
    1-800-667-5005

*Canadian Mental Health Association - New Brunswick Division*
    506-455-5231

**Prince Edward Island**

*Family Service PEI*
    1-866-892-2441

*The Island Helpline*
    1-800-218-2885

*Canadian Mental Health Association - Prince Edward Island Division*
    902-566-3034

**Nova Scotia**

*Association of Psychologists of Nova Scotia*
    902-422-9183

*Native Alcohol and Drug Abuse Counselling Association*
    1-866-588-5954

*Nova Scotia College of Counselling Therapists*
    902-225-7531

*Capital Health - Mental Health Mobile Crisis*
    1-888-429-8167

*Canadian Mental Health Association - Nova Scotia Division*
    1-888-429-8167

**Resources by territory**

**Yukon**

*Yukon Distress and Support Line*
    1-844-533-3030

*Yukon Health and Social Services*
    1-800-667-8346

## Northwest Territories

*Northwest Territories Help Line*
    1-867-767-9061

## Nunavut

*Nunavut Kamatsiaqtut Help Line*
    1-800-265-3333